PUFFIN BOOKS

THE BEWITCHING OF
ALISON ALLBRIGHT

In her imagination Alison is pretty, charming and witty, her family have a lovely house instead of the poky little unmodernised cottage they really live in, and they have parties and Mediterranean holidays. Little do her classmates know of the furious resentment which seethes inside 'Alldull', as they call her, or of the 'real' Alison who longs to get out.

Then Mrs Considine appears, like the mother of Alison's dreams, wealthy, charming and sophisticated, showering her with gifts and introducing her to the elegance and luxury for which she yearns so much. Alison is entranced with her new life, but only when it's too late does she realize the strength of the spell that Mrs Considine has cast.

In this powerful, compulsively readable story Alison is caught up in a web of make-believe that has dramatic and revelatory consequences.

Alan Davidson is the author of the five Annabel books, also published in Puffin. He is married with four children and lives in Dorset.

Other Books by Alan Davidson

JUST LIKE ANNABEL
A FRIEND LIKE ANNABEL
EVEN MORE LIKE ANNABEL
THE NEW, THINKING ANNABEL
LITTLE YEARNINGS OF ANNABEL

Alan Davidson

The Bewitching
of
Alison Allbright

PUFFIN BOOKS

PUFFIN BOOKS

Published by the Penguin Group
27 Wrights Lane, London w8 5tz, England
Viking Penguin Inc., 40 West 23rd Street, New York, New York 10010, USA
Penguin Books Australia Ltd, Ringwood, Victoria, Australia
Penguin Books Canada Ltd, 2801 John Street, Markham, Ontario, Canada l3r 1b4
Penguin Books (NZ) Ltd, 182–190 Wairau Road, Auckland 10, New Zealand

Penguin Books Ltd, Registered Offices: Harmondsworth, Middlesex, England

First published under the pen-name of A. D. Langholm by W. H. Allen 1979
This edition first published by Viking Kestrel 1988
Published in Puffin Books 1989
1 3 5 7 9 10 8 6 4 2

Reproduced, printed and bound in Great Britain by
Hazell Watson & Viney Limited
Member of BPCC Limited
Aylesbury, Bucks, England
Filmset in Linotron 202 Palatino

Contents

For Mela

1
A Staring Match

Alison knew it was stupid to have come to the lake. She ought to remount and ride away. But she didn't. She parked her bike behind some bushes and walked downhill through the trees towards the shore. There was a perfectly good track leading down from the main road, of course, but to use it would be to risk being seen.

She could hear voices and laughter ahead of her. Through the trees, the lake came into view. She halted, keeping behind cover.

Codgerley Lake was very large and studded with tree-covered islands. In the far distance, wooded slopes formed the opposite shore. It was the first really nice Saturday afternoon of the spring, sunny but fresh and sparkling, too, with enough breeze to put a glitter on the water. White and red and blue sails glided and heeled across it.

In front of Alison and slightly below her, cars and boat trailers were parked near a wooden pier to which several dinghies were moored. Some boys and girls were pushing a boat out into the water, talking and laughing together as they did so. They were all in Alison's form at Sturridge High School, except for Brian Lee who was a couple of years older and in a higher form. The boat belonged to him and his sister Kate. She was just clambering in now.

There was no sign of Raine. Perhaps she was out in one of the other boats. Or maybe she hadn't arrived yet?

Raine had been Alison's friend until she'd got mixed up with this crowd . . .

Alison looked about her. She mustn't hang about – just see if what she suspected were true and then go. She started to walk warily through the woods, moving closer to the track which led from the main road.

More voices, adult this time. She moved still more cautiously.

In a clearing amongst the trees four adults were setting up trestle tables and unpacking barbecue equipment. Alison recognized two of them as Mr and Mrs Woodward. The other couple she didn't know. They were chatting good-humouredly to each other and Alison caught some of the words:

'. . . typical, isn't it, spending our Saturday organizing a barbecue for the kids . . .'

'. . . as long as they enjoy it . . .'

'. . . only young once . . .'

So they *were* having a barbecue this evening! She'd known it. Hadn't she just known it!

The sound of a car's engine coming down the track from the main road brought back to Alison the danger of being seen. Anyway, she ought to go. Why had she submitted to this compulsion to come here? She was only hurting herself.

She turned and walked away, deliberately not looking towards the track and the car in case there were anyone she knew inside it and they happened to catch a glimpse of her through the trees.

It was a plum-coloured car driven by Raine Lawlor's mother. Raine herself was in the rear seat. She did indeed catch a glimpse of Alison through the trees. It was the merest fleeting moment, but it was enough.

'For goodness' sake!' she thought. 'That was *Alison* skulking around. Why's she being pathetic?'

It was a seven mile ride back to Alison's home on the outskirts of the small town of Sturridge Minster. She had left there an hour or so earlier, telling herself that she was simply going for a long ride because she had nothing else to do. But the lake had held a sort of magnetic attraction for her front wheel.

Alison Allbright was a slight, blue-eyed girl with dark gold hair tied in bunches. She wore it like that because such was the school rule if hair were grown further down than the collar. And Alison considered that short hair just didn't suit her at all. She was very conscious of her appearance, which she regarded as generally unsatisfactory.

Once, while waiting outside the staff room door at school, she had overheard Mrs Shearing, her English teacher, remark to someone that 'Alison Allbright would really be quite pretty if only she didn't have that morose, shrinking look on her face all the time.'

The remark had both excited and dismayed her. Could she really be pretty? Did she really look morose and shrinking? Ever since then she'd spent even more time looking in mirrors wondering if it were true and if so, what she could do about it.

It was certainly true that her normal expression was lacking in confidence, even timid, and that she never looked cheerful. At school they sometimes called her 'Allbright'n' Breezy' just because she was anything but that. 'Breezy', for short. Sometimes, 'Alldull'.

She had tried hard to cultivate a cheerful, confident expression but somehow it didn't seem to work. It merely produced a sort of tragic grimace.

But no wonder! she thought now, as she pedalled along, the breeze behind her. What did she have to be cheerful about? Look at the week that had just gone by. It had been typically rotten.

The worst thing about it had been this barbecue business. She'd been almost certain that Raine's new friends, the boaty crowd, were organizing a barbecue for this evening at Codgerley and that they'd invited most of the rest of her form at school. Almost everyone, in fact, except her. And they'd seemed to think that she wouldn't hear it being talked about at the dinner table, wouldn't cotton on.

Or, more likely, they hadn't cared. She hadn't even entered their minds.

Yet she and Raine had been friends till Raine had got mixed up with that lot. They didn't only go sailing, of course. They had a generally good time with their ponies and their parties, being chauffeured around by their doting parents. Sturridge Minster was that sort of place.

She and Raine hadn't been friends all that long but it had meant a lot to her because she wasn't used to having friends . . .

She couldn't blame Raine for dropping her, though.

'I never invite anybody back to my house,' she thought, 'never do anything that's any fun, so why should I expect people to bother about *me*?'

And Raine had tried hard to get her in with the crowd. It hadn't been her fault that it had proved impossible. If you didn't have a telephone and a car and the sort of parents willing to run you about everywhere, then you just got left behind . . .

Familiar feelings of bitterness and resentment were coursing through Alison.

'Life's so unfair. I know Mum and Dad always say they do their best but even so – oh, I suppose I ought to stop moaning.'

On the very edge of Sturridge Minster, Alison turned right into Holtwood Lane, the cul-de-sac where she lived. It was a narrow lane that almost immediately ran under a railway bridge and then swung right to run parallel with the railway embankment before petering out. It led only to a quarry, now long disused and merely a big, bumpy, rather weird hollow with stagnant pools of water. The District Council had long considered it an eyesore and had plans for an industrial estate there which never seemed to materialize, much to Alison's relief. She liked the wildness and strangeness of the quarry, where you could get away from people.

She cycled under the railway bridge and then on a sudden whim braked outside the gates of Holtwood Lodge. Getting off her bike, she wheeled it to the gates and stared over them.

Holtwood Lodge was the one really nice house in the lane, an old place with pink-washed, wisteria-clad walls, balconies at the upstairs windows and a big garden with an orchard. The same sort of house that Raine lived in. Alison liked looking at it and often, when feeling really low and resentful as she did now, she would go through a pretence that she lived there. A little dream . . . that was the best recipe for soothing herself.

It was always much the same dream. Holtwood Lodge was her home and she was returning to it now with an imaginary friend – not too imaginary, Raine, in fact – after doing a little sailing, and perhaps some riding. She had her own boat on Codgerley, the biggest on the lake. It had to be kept moored there because it was too big for even the Jaguar to trail easily round some of the bends. Raine was always welcome aboard, of course.

She had to hurry now though. 'You do remember, Raine, it's my party tonight. Mummy'll have tea waiting now and then I've got to help get things ready and dress up . . .'

Alison had a very vivid mental picture of her dream mother. Tall, cool, elegant and beautiful and wearing long white gloves.

She also had a very vivid mental picture of a dream self – the other Alison Allbright that nobody knew about, the one who was very pretty and not morose-looking at all, who captivated everyone by her charm and wit. That was the *real* Alison, just waiting to get out. She knew that was so, because she had such sparkling conversations with herself.

'I'll be seeing you tonight then, Raine. Hundreds and hundreds of people will be coming . . .'

Alison suddenly realized that she was talking out loud, as she sometimes did when having conversations with herself. Also, if the owner of Holtwood Lodge happened to come out and see her hanging over the gate like that he'd wonder what she was doing. She glanced guiltily round.

And saw Raine. Just at the very moment that Raine called out, 'Alison!'

Raine was running towards her from under the railway bridge. Beyond, her mother was getting out of the car which was parked at the corner of the main road.

The shock of seeing her here in Holtwood Lane made Alison freeze.

'I – I only just caught sight of you in time,' panted Raine,

11

halting in front of her. 'Another second and – and you'd have gone in the gate and I wouldn't have seen you.'

She was gasping for breath, smoothing back her dark hair. Alison stood transfixed. It dawned upon her that Raine was assuming that she lived in Holtwood Lodge.

'Funny!' said Raine, beginning to recover. 'I've never known where you live.' She was looking at Holtwood Lodge and was clearly surprised. 'It's a lovely place.'

If Alison were to deny it, she must do so now. But then Raine would inquisitively want to know where she did live. As she hesitated –

'Look, Alison,' said Raine. 'There's a barbecue tonight at Codgerley. I'm sorry I haven't said anything about it before. I wasn't sure you'd want to come. But would you like to?'

The excuse was weak but Raine looked so candid, so anxious to make amends, that to Alison it suddenly didn't really matter. All that mattered was that she wanted to be friends again.

Raine's mother was joining them. 'I can give you a lift there and back if I definitely know you're coming,' she said. 'I could pick you up at the corner here.'

'All right?' Raine was cajoling. 'Pick you up at quarter to seven then?'

Raine was a nice girl. Seeing Alison at the lake had given her a jolt. It had made her feel mean. She had dropped Alison, hadn't she? Maybe that was largely Alison's own fault but nevertheless it must hurt. After worrying about it for a while, Raine had asked her mother to drive towards Sturridge and catch Alison up before she disappeared in the town's traffic. They had only just managed to do so. Crazy that she didn't even know where Alison lived.

'Right, that's fine then,' said Mrs Lawlor, taking the look of dawning pleasure on Alison's face to mean assent. 'I'll just have a word with your parents and tell them what we've arranged.'

She moved towards the gate of Holtwood Lodge. She, too, believed that Alison lived there. Only the fact that Alison was effectively barring her way prevented her walking straight up the path towards the house.

A great panic instantly rose in Alison's mind.

She could, of course, tell them immediately that this wasn't her home at all. Raine would think it odd that she had let her believe it was, even momentarily, but she could bear that. What she couldn't bear, however, was the thought of leading them further along the lane, past the row of pebble-dashed 'thirties houses to the unmodernized little cottage which really was her home.

She didn't move.

'Oh, it doesn't matter about telling my mother,' she said, anguished. 'It'll be perfectly all right. I know it will.'

'But there's no harm in making sure,' said Mrs Lawlor, doubtfully. She hesitated. She was almost inclined to take Alison's word for it and turn away. But Alison was clearly hiding something.

'Yes, I really think I ought to have a quick word with your parents,' she said firmly, and started to walk round her.

'Oh, I don't want to go to the stupid barbecue,' said Alison violently. 'Leave me alone.'

'Alison – '

'What are you asking me now for?' The words came out in a sort of screech. 'Guilty conscience?'

Raine stared at her for a moment. Then she said: 'Oh, Alison, you're impossible.' She turned and started to walk back towards the car.

Her mother looked from one girl to the other helplessly, wanting to peace-make, but not sure how. Raine paused and looked back.

'Come on, Mummy,' she called. 'I'm missing the sailing.'

Mrs Lawlor looked at Alison's unyielding, stony face. 'I'm sorry you won't come,' she said awkwardly. She turned and walked back to join Raine who was getting into the car.

'What's the matter with her?' she asked Raine, puzzled, as she drove away.

'Oh, I don't know,' said Raine. 'What's it matter, any-way? I can only stand so much.'

A few minutes later, Alison stood breathing heavily in the doorway of the living room of her home.

It was a dark little room. By the single small window her

brother Keith was sitting reading. Keith was a year younger than she was and in the form below her at school, but his earnest, swotty, self-contained manner sometimes gave him the appearance of being quite grown-up. He always seemed to be indoors, even on sunny days like today. He wasn't any fun.

The room was dominated by an ancient black kitchen range, the sort of thing which had once probably been in every cottage in the district but had long ago been torn out of all the rest. Alison's mother didn't use it for cooking any longer, having a secondhand electric cooker in the scullery, but it remained there, an eyesore.

Since the room was both a sitting room and a dining room it was crammed with furniture: a square dining table firmly in the middle with dining chairs all round and two armchairs squashed between it and the kitchen range; a sideboard, and a television set on a shelf. The sheer difficulty of being able to move about the room always drove Alison wild.

Her mother was just coming in from the little scullery. She wasn't at all like Alison's dream mother. She was short, dumpy almost, with hair beginning to go grey. She had a kindly, vague face, always a little worried-looking. There was no sign of Alison's father. He was probably out on one of his long, slow walks.

'I have just lost a chance of going out to a barbecue this evening,' announced Alison. 'I have also just lost the only real friend I have ever had. And all because I was too ashamed to bring her and her mother back here. This awful, awful place!'

'Oh, Alison, don't start again,' said her mother, halting. 'Not again.'

Keith looked up from his book and groaned.

'You're a snob, Alison, that's your trouble,' he said. 'Must be miserable enough being a snob when you've got something to be snobbish about. But to be a snob when you haven't . . . you've got my sympathy.'

'It is not snobbish to want somewhere nice to live,' hissed the infuriated Alison, advancing into the room almost as if she were going to hit him. 'I just want to be like everybody

14

else. I'll put up with not having a car or a telephone or going out anywhere, but at least I'd like somewhere nice to live. We could never have a party here.'

'You're always talking about parties as if everybody else had 'em all the time – '

'*You* never have any friends. *You* never even seem to want to know anybody. You're hardly even *alive* – '

'Oh, please stop it, Alison,' pleaded her mother. 'You know we do our best.'

'You'll never understand,' shouted Alison, 'never, ever. You don't want to understand. Any of you.'

Flinging herself past her mother she stalked through the scullery and out into the back garden, slamming the door behind her. Badly wanting to make some further gesture to relieve her feelings, she gave the door a kick before turning away.

As she did so, she suddenly became aware that several pairs of curious eyes were fixed on her.

The Allbrights' back garden was small and ended at the railway embankment. It was the main London line and trains often stopped on that stretch when the signals were against them at Sturridge Junction. Alison was quite used to looking out of her bedroom window to find a row of carriages and faces unnervingly close outside.

There was a train waiting there now and several people who were gazing idly out of the window had been treated to a view of Alison's dramatic appearance through the back door. Normally she would have retreated in embarrassed silence, but now fury made her brazen and she stared back defiantly, her gaze travelling along the row of windows, seeking out each individual face and challenging it to go on looking.

The faces turned away. Back to newspapers or to staring into space. Except for one: a woman's. As Alison's gaze met hers, she continued to stare fixedly.

Alison, still in a fury, decided to outstare her. She couldn't see the woman's face very clearly through the glass of the carriage window, but she had an impression of it being aloof and authoritative. Probably somebody smart and well-off wondering what sort of lives were led by the sub-humans in the scruffy cottages by the railway line. But surely she wouldn't have the nerve to keep it up much longer . . . what was the matter with her?

The train slid almost silently into motion. But now the woman was turning her head so as to be able to keep Alison in view . . .

It was Alison who, unable to endure it any longer, dropped her eyes. The woman kept on staring at her until she was lost to sight.

She was a woman in her late thirties or perhaps early forties, seated alone in a first class, non-smoking compartment. She wore a very expensive light grey suit with green trimmings and the luggage on the rack above her was of the very best quality.

She bore, indeed, a surprising resemblance to the mental picture that Alison had when she thought of her dream mother. She was tall, elegant, could certainly be described as beautiful and, although she didn't wear long white gloves, she would have looked very well in them if she had.

When, soon afterwards, she got out of the train at Sturridge Minster station she was met by a young, uniformed chauffeur who saluted her respectfully and gravely before taking her luggage and escorting her to the waiting car.

'It's nice to see you back, Mrs Considine,' he said.

'Thank you, Michael,' she replied.

He saw that she was abstracted and, indeed, looked rather pale, but he didn't comment because he thought he knew the reason. He was wrong. He didn't.

The lives of Alison and Mrs Considine had touched. At a distance; through a glass; but they had touched.

2
The Distinguished Departure of a Bicycle

They were talking about the barbecue at school on Monday. Apparently it had been a good one. Alison listened to the gossip about it as she ate her lunch silently. No one seemed to remember that she hadn't been invited. Probably they'd never even thought about it.

Alison hated break periods, whether mid-morning or lunch, because she had to spend them alone and she was painfully conscious that her isolation was obvious to everyone. But most of all she hated this time when she was sitting down having lunch. She was naturally shy with people she didn't know well and since she never did anything of interest she had nothing to talk about. She just sat there hoping no one would notice her, especially Stephen Kirkpatrick, whom she dreaded. He was a tall, gangling, loose-mouthed boy who sat directly opposite her, a slightly sardonic grin almost perpetually on his face.

Jenny Allingham was leading the chat about the barbecue. She'd obviously had a marvellous time there. It had been, as she put it, 'raveworthy'.

Jenny Allingham sat directly across the table from Alison and was one of those people who made Alison feel particularly small, squashed and useless. She could ski, ride a horse, sail a boat and skate and she did all these things regularly. She wasn't long back from the school's annual skiing trip to Austria and she often went away at weekends to do grass skiing. It was somewhere quite far off but, of course, her parents didn't mind driving her there.

17

The whole business of the school's skiing trip made Alison feel resentful and envious. For a week during term time some of the people in her form disappeared, with the games master, to the Alps. But if Alison had asked for a day off to go on a bike ride it wouldn't have been allowed.

Then Jenny, like most of the rest of them, would go off for another holiday in the summer with her parents, usually to somewhere exotic. Alison had once had to endure a prolonged discussion, led by Jenny, as to which Mediterranean country had the least polluted beaches. What an excuse for showing off that had provided! It had made Alison feel quite sick. The places people had been to! And Jenny seemed to have been to the lot!

Of course there were some who, like Alison, didn't appear to have been anywhere. It didn't seem to bother them all that much, but it bothered her. It was bad enough to have been born into a hard-up and boring family but why did it have to be in Sturridge Minster where everyone else was well-off and to which people actually moved because of its 'superb little school', 'not like that giant, sprawling thing over at Shamfield', 'oh, that's an appalling place . . .'

Alison's holidays usually consisted of going to stay for a week or two with Aunt Lucy and Uncle Jeff who lived in Yorkshire, very handy, supposedly, for Scarborough and Bridlington – which it would have been if they'd had a car – and, afterwards, Aunt Lucy and Uncle Jeff would come to them. Alison's parents had lived in Yorkshire before moving south.

Actually, though she didn't like admitting it to herself, Alison did quite enjoy those holidays. They were the only times, too, when she and Keith seemed to have anything much to say to each other. They'd go for long walks together over the North Yorkshire Moors, following streams up to their sources. But going off to stay with relatives . . . She would never admit that to Jenny Allingham.

And thinking of Keith, she could see him now at one of the other tables; just his rather hunched back as he concentrated on his meal. He looked so absolutely self-contained, as usual, so totally unconscious of everybody else. He didn't seem to suffer from all the fears and grievances which occupied her mind so much of the time. Nor did he seem to attract any teasing or tormenting as she did. Nobody bothered with him.

'What a pudding!' Alison thought fiercely. 'He hardly even *exists*.' It should have been so nice to have a brother at the same school. They ought to have been able to help each other, lean on each other, especially as they both had so much difficulty in making friends. But it didn't work out like that at all. In fact, Alison tended to avoid him because she was rather ashamed of him. Boring, self-contained little swot! The Allbrights must look a bit pathetic to everyone, they really must –

Alison suddenly felt guilty. She always seemed to be thinking these mean thoughts about her family. She really oughtn't to. It was having to sit and listen to them going on about the barbecue that was making her feel so bitter.

Though it was the truth she was thinking about her family, wasn't it? Only the truth. No one could blame her for thinking that.

Think about something else though. Something nice . . .

There had been a Rolls-Royce in Holtwood Lane yesterday evening.

She had noticed it when going to the corner shop on her bike to get some matches for her mother. It had been parked right at the end of the lane, by the quarry beyond their house and on the opposite side, pointing in their direction. It looked as if someone were sitting behind the wheel but she couldn't be sure.

It had been such an amazing sight in Holtwood Lane that she'd wanted to go and look at it. It had looked so inviting, dark blue and all lustrous from having been polished so many times. She would have liked to touch it.

But since there might have been somebody inside it, she'd had to refrain from staring rudely and instead content herself with wondering what it was doing there and having little day-dreams that it was someone looking for her. Some long-lost, wealthy uncle . . .

It had gone when she returned from the corner shop.

But *what* had it been doing in the lane? Someone searching for Holtwood Lodge, maybe?

Alison became aware that she was being spoken to by Stephen Kirkpatrick.

'Hey – Bright'n' Breezy – quiet, aren't you? Whatcha thinking about?'

He was off again. He seemed to take a malevolent delight in asking strings of unanswerable questions. It was why she dreaded him so much. What *was* she supposed to say?

'What have *you* been doing over the weekend? Everybody else has said, so what about you?'

If she had been able to summon up some sort of repartee, however feeble, she would probably have been able to shake him off. But she couldn't. She just sat there, timidly blushing. The sight seemed to give him some sort of pleasure.

'Didn't see you at the barbecue. Had another engagement, did you?'

It was lucky that the prefect was rising at the end of the table and she could rise thankfully, too. Where, oh where, was that sparkling, vivacious Alison who was so popular and had everyone flocking around her . . . the Alison of her day-dreams?

Afterwards, Alison went for a walk round the school grounds. She could have gone to the library to read but it was too pleasant a day not to want to be outside and anyway, Keith would almost certainly be there. He always was at lunch times, often by himself. The thought of two Allbrights sitting like lemons in the library was too nasty even to think about.

But it wasn't a great deal better out in the grounds. Everywhere there were groups wandering about chatting or playing ball games. Raine was in one of the groups together with Kate Lee and Janet Dimlow and Susannah Strickland and some other girls. They were chatting to some of the boys. Coming upon them as she turned a corner, Alison had to pause abruptly and change direction so as not to barge into the midst of them. She didn't want to catch Raine's eye because she wouldn't have known whether to smile and say hallo or simply look away again.

Nor did she want to be seen looking pathetic by Susannah Strickland.

Susannah was another enemy, the principal enemy, beside whom Stephen Kirkpatrick faded to comparatively harmless insignificance. Susannah, very pretty and self-possessed, had always treated Alison with unconcealed contempt, usually looking through her as if she didn't even exist. But, above all, it was Susannah who had taken Raine away from her.

Alison had fantasies about getting her own back. In these fantasies her father had won a fortune on the football pools and they were now living in Holtwood Lodge. They were having the most fantastic party to which everybody had been invited. Everyone, that is, except Susannah Strickland. Even Stephen Kirkpatrick had been invited so that Alison could be coolly and condescendingly gracious to him. As she went to the window to draw the long velvet curtains, Alison would catch a glimpse of Susannah hanging forlornly around outside, hoping for a last-minute change of heart on Alison's part and an invitation inside. Alison would draw the curtains on her.

It wasn't a very satisfactory fantasy, however. For one thing, Alison's father didn't do the football pools. And for another she had the feeling that even if he did and won a fortune, the look on Susannah's face would probably become even more distantly contemptuous. In Susannah's world only common people, undesirable to know, won money on the pools and then flaunted their wealth. She wouldn't want to go to their parties. With someone like Susannah, there was no way of winning.

Oh, well! It hadn't been much of a day so far. Perhaps something nice would happen this afternoon.

She didn't expect it would.

It didn't – not while she was at school, anyway. Something rather nasty happened instead.

The last lesson of the day was history, taken by Mr Craig, who was also the form master. At the end of the lesson he brought up the subject of the form's outing on the following Saturday.

Now Alison hated school outings anyway. Outings to

anywhere. This was for the simple reason that she was never able to go on them. But at least when she didn't go on, say, the school skiing expedition, she was part of the majority who didn't go either. The Bransome Park outing was infinitely worse because she was the only one, yes, the only one in the form not going.

It had first been brought to the form's attention a few weeks previously. A series of charity concerts, with stars from stage and television, was to be held at Bransome Park, a 'stately home' some forty miles from Sturridge Minster and the school's Parent-Teachers Association had offered to arrange block bookings and transport if there was a sufficient number who wanted to go.

The response had been overwhelming. Every single person in the form, except for Alison, had put his or her name down.

Alison had pleaded with her parents to let her go but her father had told her that they weren't able to afford luxuries at present. He couldn't, in any case, see why she wanted to go. They had a television set, didn't they? Weren't there enough stars on that?

The first feelings of bitter resentment had died down by now, but here was Mr Craig raising the subject again to check that there were no last-minute withdrawals or additions and to remind everyone that payment was now due.

'Let's see,' he said, looking vaguely around the classroom, 'the simplest thing is for all those who are going to raise their hands.'

A forest of hands went up.

'Seems to be everyone,' he said. He had clearly forgotten that Alison wasn't going. 'Is that so? Let's make sure by asking anyone who *isn't* going to raise a hand.'

Alison's hand inched up. And only Alison's . . .

'Oh, yes,' he said, looking down the list, 'I remember now. Of course, Alison Allbright.'

He was too absorbed in his list to see the expression on Alison's face.

But then he didn't notice Alison much, anyway. On the rare occasions when he did, it was merely to reflect that she rather got on his nerves, always sitting there silently, always looking downbeat, always somewhere near the bottom of the class without being obviously inattentive. He'd rather have the unruly ones any day. At least you had a chance of getting through to them.

He would have been amazed to know of the emotions that raged through Alison's mind as, soon afterwards, she got her bike out of the shed. She had never felt quite so dejected, bitter and alone as this.

She rode, brooding, along Eastgate Street and turned left into Sturridge's broad, beautiful – almost too beautiful – High Street with its antique shops and inns so smartened up they looked artificial. At the end of the High Street she bore right into Ardington Road.

Alison always cycled to school and back although she could have got a place on the school bus, as Keith did, if she'd really wanted to. Strictly speaking, their home wasn't outside the walking limit so he wasn't entitled to a bus place, but since there were several spare seats no one minded.

Alison, however, preferred the freedom of the bike instead of having to join the queue with, among others, Stephen Kirkpatrick who also lived in her direction, in one of the villages outside Sturridge. She was altogether keen on her bike. It meant a lot to her since the family had no car. It was very old and rusty now, having been passed on to her by her mother who had herself used it when she was Alison's age, but Alison didn't mind that. She was just thankful she had it.

A little way along the Ardington Road was a parade of shops which included a newsagent's and confectioner's where Alison sometimes stopped to buy a lemon or orange drink if she had sufficient pocket money. Feeling in her pocket, she decided that she had enough now. It was a warm afternoon and, more important, she wanted to put off going home for a few more minutes.

It was a high kerb and Alison stood her bike against it, using the pedal to prop it up. Then she went into the shop.

There were other customers in there, waiting patiently while an old gentleman settled his paper bill. Alison joined the queue. She was still preoccupied with the barbecue, with Raine, with Susannah Strickland, with the concert at Bransome Park . . .

From outside came a crash. Lost in her thoughts it took a moment or two for it to dawn on Alison that it was the sound of her bike falling over. Simply assuming that she had not propped it up securely, she started towards the door, only to realize as she did so that the sound of the crash was being followed by a dragging, scrunching noise.

When she opened the shop door she saw that a Rolls-Royce was parked outside. A chauffeur was just getting out. Curiously, it looked very like the Rolls-Royce that had been in Holtwood Lane on the previous evening.

But more important than that for the moment was that her bike now lay on the road beneath the car's rear wheels. It had been run over and was contorted beyond repair.

3
The Coming of
Mrs Considine

The bike had been the only thing that Alison had felt she could really count on. A spasm of real grief passed through her.

The chauffeur came towards her.

'Is it your bike?' he asked. Alison nodded, dumbly.

He was quite good-looking, young with a shrewd, alert face above which his chauffeur's peaked cap was perched very slightly to one side, giving him the merest hint of rakishness. Otherwise his uniform was immaculate.

'I'm very sorry about it,' he said. 'It was entirely my fault. I didn't see it there but I ought to have done.'

He turned and, hitching up his trousers, stooped to examine the bike.

'It was pretty old and rusty, wasn't it,' he said, soothingly. 'Don't you worry. As it was my fault it'll be replaced with a nice new one.'

He stood up, opened the boot of the Rolls-Royce, then picked up the mangled bike and put it inside. Alison watched the lid close on it.

'You won't be wanting that any longer, will you,' he said.

Had it really disappeared from her life forever, after being a part of it for so long? What an extraordinary way to go, flattened beneath the wheels of a Rolls-Royce! Quite a distinguished way, really . . .

She was already feeling better, relieved by his ready

acceptance of blame and excited by the promise of a new bike.

He wiped his hands, and the boot handle, with a handkerchief, then reached into his inside pocket and took out a ball-point pen and notebook, which he opened.

'What's your name and address?' he asked her. 'I really am sorry about this.'

'You mean it about getting me a new bike?' said Alison, when she'd told him. She couldn't quite believe that he'd be so casual about it.

'Of course,' he said, still writing. 'Or, at any rate, my employer will. She's very good about anything like this and – ' he nodded towards the car and smiled ' – as you can see, she can afford to be.'

He was writing something else besides her name and address. When he'd finished, he tore the page out of the notebook and handed it to her. Underneath the date he had written:

To Miss Alison Allbright:

I accept full responsibility for the damage to your bicycle which was entirely due to my negligence. I also accept that it is a write-off and promise to replace it at the earliest possible opportunity.

It was signed: *Michael Housman, Rosewilder, Sturridge Minster*.

'Good enough?' he said, encouragingly.

'Yes,' said Alison. 'Thank you.'

'Then perhaps I can give you a lift home now.'

Alison looked at the Rolls-Royce. She was beginning to enjoy this. It had brought a little excitement into her life and she was dying to ride in that car.

Then she shook her head sadly. 'No, thank you,' she said. 'I haven't far to walk now.'

It had long been impressed upon Alison by her mother that she must never accept lifts from strangers and however much she might rebel against her parents in her imagination, she didn't really do so in practice.

Besides, it was dawning upon her that there was a slight feeling of oddness about this whole incident. It was curious, though no more than that perhaps, that she had noticed a dark blue Rolls-Royce near her house yesterday and now here was an identical one running over her bike. But it was also coming back to her how long it had seemed from the moment she had first heard the bike fall over to the time he had stopped moving backwards over it. He must have been in a dream, or maybe a Rolls was so insulated from outside noise and bumps that he hadn't known about it. Yes, that might be the answer. To think for even a moment that he had run over the bike deliberately was obviously ludicrous . . . It was very lucky for him that the bike hadn't fallen against the car and scratched it.

She wondered whether she should ask if it were his car that had been in the lane, but she didn't get the chance.

'Well, goodbye, and sorry again,' he said. 'You'll have a new bike very soon, though.' He started to get back into the car, then smiled and got out again.

'I almost forgot what I stopped for in the first place,' he said. 'Some chocolate. Goodbye.'

'Bye,' said Alison.

She watched him as he disappeared into the news-agent's. Two or three people who had come out of the shop to see what had happened went back inside, too. Alison set off to walk home. She wouldn't bother about the drink now.

The Rolls-Royce passed her well before she got to Holt-wood Lane, but the chauffeur didn't appear to see her. Funny to think of her bike disappearing in that resplendent boot! She wondered if Rosewilder lay in that direction. It depended, of course, whether he were coming from it or going towards it. She wasn't even sure what Rosewilder was. A house? Or a street?

She wondered, too, who his employer was, this person, 'she', who could so easily afford to be so good about things.

To have touched this person's life, even so remotely, made Alison feel quite glamorous. She began to wonder if the bike would be delivered to the house in the Rolls-Royce.

It was odd though. Odd but quite exciting. Yes, on

second thoughts, something nice had happened this afternoon.

'Rosewilder?' said Alison's father scathingly. 'Have you ever heard of it, Keith? I haven't.'

Keith, who was sitting by the window as usual, shook his head.

'It must be a house,' he said. 'There isn't any street called that in Sturridge.'

'It's probably nothing at all,' said Mr Allbright. 'It probably doesn't exist.'

He was sitting at the table with Alison's mother having his evening meal after getting home from work. Alison and Keith had already had theirs.

He was a big, slow-moving man. Looking at him, you would never have guessed that he spent all day packing little parcels for a small mail order firm in Sturridge Minster. He had been a bricklayer once but he'd had to give that up and get light indoor work because of rheumatism.

'But he wouldn't make it up,' said Alison desperately. 'Why should he? His employer's got pots of money. He said so.'

Alison was standing by the table, her hands gripping the back of a chair. She'd had a bad time since arriving back home. Her mother had been upset by the loss of the bicycle and apparently quite unable to grasp that it was going to be replaced by a shining new one. Now her father, who was usually so patient, was being very irritable with her.

'His employer might have plenty of money,' he said, 'but it wasn't his employer who ran over the bike. It was him. You've got nothing but his word for it that anybody's going to pay – '

'His note – ' began Alison.

'Did he show you any proof that that was his real name and address?'

'No,' said Alison, with a sinking heart.

'Did you take his car number?'

'No,' said Alison. '*No*.'

'Oh, don't go on at her,' said her mother. 'I'm upset about the bike but it wasn't Alison's fault. You can't think

28

of everything, can you, dear? And I don't know what you're going to do now. Even second-hand bikes are expensive. It's not like the days when you could pick one up for a pound or two.'

Her mother's words of support and sympathy seemed more depressing to Alison at that moment than her father's criticism. Maybe she had been a fool. Maybe she would never see that chauffeur again. She'd let him get rid of her with a meaningless note and then drive away. But was there any need to be so downbeat?

'And I suppose,' she said, turning abruptly away from the table, 'that if we can't get one for a pound or two that means I'll never have another bike.'

'Now don't start on about money again, Alison,' said her mother. 'You know we're not made of it. If you need things you ought to try and get jobs yourself – '

'I've *tried* to get jobs,' said Alison. 'There aren't many round Sturridge and when there is one, what happens? Somebody gets it whose parents have put in a word for them. Somebody who probably doesn't even need the money – '

'Now, Alison – ' began her father, but she wasn't listening. She was staring at a typewritten note which was gathering dust propped up against the back of the sideboard. It was the original notification from the school, now some weeks old, of the outing to Bransome Park. It brought back with a rush all the bitterness she had felt that afternoon. She looked round.

'I had to put my hand up in class today as the only one not going to Bransome Park,' she said in a voice that quivered. 'As if that wasn't enough for one day it looks as if I mightn't even have a bike – '

Her voice was rising, getting more out of control.

'If you're going to talk like that,' said her father, curtly, 'you can go to your room.'

She looked at him for a moment without speaking, then turned and walked out of the door, slamming it behind her. She stamped up the stairs.

'Alison,' called her mother. She started after her, but was stopped by a look from Mr Allbright.

29

'Let her sulk if she wants to,' he said, still curtly. He transferred his gaze to his newspaper.

Keith turned a page of his book.

'I'm not going to Bransome Park, either,' he mumbled. '*And* I haven't got a bike of my own.'

'What did you say, Keith?' asked his mother.

'Nothing,' he said and went on reading.

Mrs Allbright sank down into a chair and put her hands to her face, while upstairs Alison sat on her bed in a fury and watched a train go by, rumbling over the points. It reminded her for a moment of the woman who had stared at her so persistently on Saturday evening.

Alison went to school on the bus next day. The journey there passed uneventfully, but on the way back in the afternoon Stephen Kirkpatrick got hold of her bag and he and Simon Howarth started tossing it backwards and forwards to each other, and her homework books and PE kit and plimsolls all fell out and were scattered over the floor. Jill Mackenzie, who was in the sixth form, was furious with the boys and told them off, insisting that they pick everything up again, which they did, chuckling and passing comments all the time.

Alison was almost as embarrassed by Jill Mackenzie's intervention as by what the boys had done, but nevertheless she was very grateful. Acts of kindness towards her always made Alison's heart well over with gratitude and a desire to do something in return. She decided that when her father won the football pools, Jill Mackenzie, who was now immersed in her book again, would be at the top of the list of those who would find that their good deeds did not go unrewarded . . .

Keith, of course, hadn't helped at all. But that was just as well.

Life was going to be impossible without her bike. It was only just dawning upon her *how* impossible. She had given up any hope of its being replaced. She'd never see that chauffeur again.

She felt a sense of desolation and loss that evening such as she had never known before. When her father got back from work he started on about whether they should go and tell the police about the bike, or whether there was any point since she didn't even know the car's number. Alison couldn't summon up the energy to care. She went upstairs and sat in her room again, so as to get out of the way and have some peace.

It wasn't only the bike. It was Raine. It was everything.

She didn't hear the knock at the front door. She just heard her mother's mystified voice calling, 'Alison – Alison – it's somebody for you, love.'

No one had ever called at the house for her. She'd never wanted anybody to. As she opened the door and started down the stairs she couldn't imagine whom she was going to see.

A woman stood on the doorstep. She was wearing a pale beige summer coat, her hands thrust casually into the big pockets. She stood very easily and elegantly, as fashion models do when they're showing off clothes, but in her case quite unconsciously. She had dark brown hair falling around an oval face with a high forehead. She was really quite beautiful and she exuded a restless dynamism. She was probably not a great deal younger than Alison's mother who stood awkwardly by her, but the contrast was quite unbelievable. In her presence the Allbrights' front door, the hall and the staircase all looked unutterably squalid.

Seeing Alison coming wide-eyed down the stairs towards her, she showed white teeth in a smile.

'Alison!' she said. 'I'm so glad I've found you.'

Her voice was beautiful, too. It was authoritative and, without actually having any accent, it had that burr, that certain quality of cultivated upperclassness, which is picked up only in the very best places.

As Alison came down into the hall she saw that the Rolls-Royce was parked outside and that the chauffeur was opening the gate and pushing through it a gleaming new bicycle.

The woman held out a hand which Alison took limply.

'I've just been introducing myself to your mother,' she said. 'I am Mrs Considine.'

4
A Crucial Decision

No one replied. Alison's mother continued to stare self-consciously. Mr Allbright appeared in the doorway from the sitting room clutching a newspaper in one hand, also staring. Even in the midst of her amazement, Alison was conscious of how awkward, how churlish the Allbrights' welcome must seem and was ashamed.

But Mrs Considine didn't seem to notice. 'I do hope I'm not intruding,' she said, directing her smile towards Mr Allbright now, 'but I felt I had to come and tell Alison personally how sorry I was about her bike. I expect she's been missing it dreadfully.'

She looked at Mr Allbright for only a moment, then her gaze went back to Alison. She had hardly taken her eyes off Alison since first seeing her. She was still holding her hand.

Alison was fascinated by Mrs Considine's smile. Beginning with a display of white teeth it then settled down into a different sort of smile, the mouth elongating more at one side than the other, the lips quirking, a quite girlishly eager smile.

'Come and see your new bike,' she said, releasing Alison's hand at last, 'and tell me if it makes up for Michael's being so clumsy.'

For the first time, Alison experienced a thrill of excitement and relief. Her father had been wrong, after all. The chauffeur – 'Michael' – had meant everything he had said! He was now standing behind his employer, holding the new bike.

'I don't expect you'll have any complaints,' he said to her

32

as she stepped down on to the garden path to look at it. 'It's got five speeds and a carrier and speedometer and mileage recorder – '

'Speedometer!' exclaimed Alison. 'Mileage recorder!'

She'd never imagined she'd own a bike with those sorts of refinements.

'Try it out,' said Mrs Considine.

Alison noticed that Keith had appeared in the hall and was standing there watching. All she could think about now, however, was riding the bike. The chauffeur held the gate open for her as she wheeled it out into the lane and then mounted it.

It made her realize that she'd never ridden a decent bike before. When riding the old one, she'd always had the feeling that she was holding it together while doing so. The wheels had never felt very secure. The brake blocks had sometimes rubbed against the wheel rims, the saddle had slipped and wobbled however securely the nuts had been tightened. She had grown so used to these, and other defects, that they had become part of her life, almost unnoticed. But how different, how superb this bike was in comparison, gliding smoothly along, everything solid and firm and reliable. It was the nicest thing she had ever had.

At the bend in the lane she turned and rode back to the house. The chauffeur was standing by the car now. Keith had come outside the door. Mrs Considine, still smiling, was standing by the gate with her parents.

'Like it?' asked Mrs Considine, as Alison halted in front of her.

Still too overwhelmed and shy to speak, Alison nodded. She couldn't believe her luck. That of all the bikes in the world he had chosen *hers* to run over! Luck like that just didn't happen to her. Extraordinary, fantastic luck!

Then she saw the expressions on her parents' faces. They both looked worried.

'Alison can't take that!' said her mother. 'Her old bike wasn't anything like as good as that.'

'It was just an old wreck,' said her father.

Alison wanted to explode. Why couldn't her parents just accept the luck that had come her way? There was this Mrs

Considine in her coat worth hundreds of pounds with her Rolls-Royce and chauffeur beside her. The cost of the bike meant nothing to her. Nothing. It was fine to be honest and scrupulous. She always tried to be honest and scrupulous herself. But why did her parents always take it to such extremes? Always. Give them half a chance and they'd ruin everything . . .

But Mrs Considine simply laughed. She was still watching Alison whose hands had tightened instinctively on the handlebars.

'I hope you're not suggesting I take it away again,' she said. 'I really wouldn't know what to do with it now. My own cycling days are over, I'm afraid.'

'Thank you,' said Alison sincerely.

There was a silence. Mr and Mrs Allbright didn't know what else to say and nor did Alison. She was expecting that Mrs Considine would now, her duty done, breathe a sigh of relief and get into her car, anxious to escape as quickly as possible back to her, doubtless, infinitely more desirable normal surroundings at Rosewilder, wherever that was.

But instead Mrs Considine turned to Alison's mother. 'I wonder if you could offer me a cup of tea,' she said. 'I'm simply dying for one.'

Alison was suddenly filled with shame again. Nobody had thought to offer hospitality. She shouldn't have had to ask herself. Why were the Allbrights always so clueless, never knowing what to do or how to behave themselves in any situation?

'Oh, yes,' said Mrs Allbright, surprised and flustered. 'You'll have to take us as we are, though. Our house isn't grand.'

'I'm not concerned whether your house is grand or not,' smiled Mrs Considine.

Alison's father looked hesitantly at the chauffeur.

'What about you – would you – ?' he began.

'Would you like some tea, Michael?' asked Mrs Considine.

He shook his head. 'No thanks. I'll wait in the car,' he said.

Alison carefully parked her new bike against the wall of the house and followed the others inside.

It was very strange to see Mrs Considine, after pleasantly saying hallo to Keith and asking him if he were Alison's brother, to which he replied with a shy nod, step into the hall and through into the living room. Mrs Allbright fussed around her, pulling a chair out from under the table, even pushing the table over a little way to give more room between it and the sideboard.

If it had been any other visitor Alison would have been dying of shame several times over. But with Mrs Considine it didn't seem to matter. Her world was so far removed from theirs that the ordinary standards didn't apply.

She sat down elegantly on the dining chair with the frayed seat, so elegantly that she made the room seem even smaller, shabbier and more tasteless than it usually did to Alison. While Mrs Allbright went to make tea she made conversation with Alison's father who stood awkwardly in front of the fireplace, his back slightly bent because of his rheumatism. She professed to admire the black kitchen range, saying how solid it looked and what a pity it was that there were so few left nowadays. Mr Allbright simply listened, not knowing what to reply.

Alison was standing by the window with Keith by her side. She was wondering why Mrs Considine had wanted to come inside. She could smell her perfume. It was subtly, deliciously haunting. It must be very expensive.

She was fascinated by Mrs Considine. Never before had she been so close to anyone who exuded such glamour, who had about them such an aura of wealth and authority.

She noticed that although Mrs Considine was talking to her father, her gaze kept on coming back to her, Alison.

Seeing Mrs Considine's head turned towards her like that, Alison had a sudden feeling of having seen her before. But where . . .?

Outside, a diesel train roared by.

The person on the train! The person who had outstared her!

No. That would be ridiculous.

Mrs Allbright brought in the tea. It was in the china cups

with the wavy rims and the little roses painted on them which Alison had never expected to be actually used. She thought they looked ridiculous on a metal tray with pictures of bottles of beer on it.

She sipped the tea self-consciously, as did the rest of her family, while Mrs Considine chatted to them, asking Alison and Keith questions about their school, urging Mrs Allbright to sit down, which she seemed disinclined to do, and generally seeming to play the role of hostess rather than guest.

When she had finished her tea she rose to her feet.

'That was very nice,' she said. 'Thank you, Mrs Allbright. And now before I go there is just one more thing.'

She looked at Alison, who was still standing by the window. 'I feel so guilty that you've been without your bike. You must have been so upset by it all and I'd like to make up for that.'

She turned to Alison's parents, looking from one to the other.

'Would you mind if I took Alison out for a treat – some sort of outing?'

Alison's heart leapt.

'You mean in the Rolls-Royce?' she said, quickly.

Mrs Considine laughed. 'Yes, if you like,' she said.

'But you've already bought her a new bike – ' began Mrs Allbright.

'Stop it, mum!' thought Alison. 'Stop it, stop it, *stop it*!'

'But I'd feel so guilty if I didn't,' said Mrs Considine. 'Tell me, Alison, where would you like to go? A film, perhaps, or to tea somewhere – '

She paused and Alison saw that she was looking at the notice about the school outing which was still propped up against the back of the sideboard.

'So you're going to the concert at Bransome Park!' she said.

'No,' said Alison. Despite all this quite breathtaking excitement, her bitterness about the outing remained. 'We can't *afford* it.'

She would never have dreamed of saying that to anyone

36

outside the family normally, but Mrs Considine was different.

'You mean,' said Mrs Considine, looking at her, 'that you'd *like* to go?'

'I'd like to go very much,' said Alison. She glanced at her parents and repeated: 'But we can't *afford* it.'

'Then that's where I shall take you for your outing,' said Mrs Considine, 'with, of course, the permission of your parents.'

She turned and smiled her fascinating smile at Mr and Mrs Allbright.

'But – but it's forty miles away!' said Alison, astounded.

'Forty miles?' said Mrs Considine, in a tone of voice which implied that she couldn't quite see what that had to do with anything.

'It's all booked up.'

'I think that could be arranged,' said Mrs Considine.

Alison's heart was suddenly leaping.

'I'd love to go there. *Love* to.'

'Then you shall,' smiled Mrs Considine. 'We'll consider it a date, shall we – '

It was all unbelievable. Unbelievable!

'Just a minute,' said Alison's father. 'We seem to be moving a bit fast.'

The tone of his voice made Alison's heart plummet. He was looking quite bewildered.

'You've given Alison a marvellous new bike,' he said. 'Far better than the old one. She's very grateful for that and so are we all. That's quite enough. You don't need to take her out anywhere.'

'But I'd like to – ' began Mrs Considine.

'No, Mrs Considine, you've done quite enough.' His voice was flat and definite.

Mrs Considine looked at him as if about to argue, but then she seemed to realize that there was no point.

'Very well, Mr Allbright,' she said. 'If you really don't want me to, then of course I shan't. But I shall be left feeling guilty.'

She was still smiling. But Alison, even in the midst of the anguish she felt at that moment, thought there was something strange about the smile. It was too bright. It was as if Mrs Considine were really deeply affected and disappointed and trying to hide it. Whereas that clearly could not be the case.

'It's very nice to have met you all,' she said, and held out a hand to each one of them in turn. She came to Alison last.

'Goodbye, Alison,' she said, and that strange bright smile was still on her face.

Alison's anguish was unbounded as, through the window, she watched her go out through the gate, saw the chauffeur open the car door for her.

And then Alison exploded.

'Why do you have to ruin everything,' she shouted. 'Everything.'

'Alison,' said her father, 'I'm not going to let you be taken forty miles away by a total stranger who appears out of the blue.'

'You never give me anything yourself and you stop anybody else giving me anything.'

'Stop shouting, Alison. You've just been given a brand new bike. Why couldn't she just leave it at that? What did she want to take you out for? Why did she keep on staring at you?'

'Why does everybody have to be so *suspicious* all the time? Some people are just generous. *You* as good as told me I'd never see that chauffeur again. You were wrong. *Wrong!*'

'Alison!' said her mother. 'Stop being so rude to your father or you can go outside. You're never satisfied, are you? Whatever you're given, you always want more.'

Alison watched with helpless despair as the Rolls-Royce slid away down Holtwood Lane. Mrs Considine didn't look back.

Suddenly, in a blind rage, she stormed out of the room. Through the scullery and out through the back door, slamming it behind her. She stood in the back garden, head bowed, hands clenched.

Of course the bike was marvellous. But she had been offered a glimpse of something even more wonderful.

'Oh, Alison!' said her mother despairingly. She made as if to follow her.

'Leave her alone,' said her father irritably. He sat down and picked up his paper again. Mrs Allbright hesitated, then reluctantly sat down too. Keith resumed his seat by the window.

Outside, Alison suddenly looked up towards the railway embankment. She had just thought of something.

Mrs Considine's car would by now be nearing the bend in Holtwood Lane. After turning the bend, it would pass under the railway bridge and head towards the main road. When it got there the car could either turn right towards the town, or left away from it.

If it turned left the car would soon pass along the road on the other side of the embankment, opposite to where Alison was now standing. So that, if she wanted to intercept it and see Mrs Considine again before she disappeared for ever, all she had to do was to get over the fence at the bottom of the garden, climb the embankment, cross the tracks, scramble down the other side . . .

But why would she want to see Mrs Considine again?

To tell her that her parents had changed their minds and were willing to let her go on the outing after all?

But that would be a lie

A decision was crystallizing in Alison's mind. It was a terrifying one because she had never before defied her parents' wishes in anything that really mattered, or told a really big lie. She knew that if she did so now, life could never be quite the same again.

Should she? She stood poised in an agony of doubt, knowing that in a matter of seconds the decision would be out of her hands. Whether the car turned right or left at the main road would be of no consequence. Whichever way it went it would have gone out of reach for ever.

Suddenly, she knew what she was going to do. She was going to leave it to Fate. She would try to intercept the car. But if she couldn't because the car turned the other way, then she would know that she wasn't meant to . . .

She glanced behind her at the rear windows of the house. There was no one watching her. She ran.

It was a board fence at the bottom of the garden but there were pieces missing and it was quite easy to scramble over. She plunged down on the other side and ran up the embankment.

It was strange and for some reason rather frightening to be up on top of it. She looked along the tracks which stabbed their way to the horizon. There was nothing coming and she darted across, down the other side, over another fence. She was in a narrow strip of dense woodland which divided the railway line from the main road. Ahead she could hear the drone and swish of cars. It seemed ages since she'd left the garden. Surely she must have missed Mrs Considine anyway! Perhaps it would be better if she had.

She pushed her way through a tangle of branches to find that only a barbed wire fence lay between her and the grass verge of the main road. She pulled the top two strands apart and climbed through.

She stood, panting, on the verge. Cars were passing but there was no sign of the Rolls-Royce. Had she missed it or – ?

A gleaming car bonnet appeared some distance away to her right. It was the Rolls, just coming out of Holtwood Lane. It halted to let a car go past, then started to nose foward into the main road. Alison froze. Which way would it turn? Left or right.

It turned left towards her, began to accelerate, then slowed as the chauffeur saw her standing by the edge of the road. It came to a halt and the rear window slid somehow magically downwards and Mrs Considine was smiling at her again.

'Why, Alison!' she said. 'How did you get here?'

'I took a short cut.' Alison was still panting. 'Mum and Dad told me to run after you – say they were sorry – hoped they weren't rude – it will be all right for me to go to Bransome Park. If – if you still want me to.'

'Of course!' said Mrs Considine. 'I'm delighted – really delighted. Do thank them for me.'

'Yes – yes, I will,' said Alison.

'So shall I pick you up at your house immediately after

lunch on Saturday – or would you prefer to meet some-where?'

'I'd rather meet you somewhere, if you don't mind,' said Alison. 'Would it be all right if I waited at – ' she glanced up and down the road searching for inspiration. 'There's the big pillar box outside the main post office – '

'I know it,' said Mrs Considine. 'We'll see you there . . . Two o'clock on Saturday? Good. Till then.'

The window slid up again and Alison watched as the car gathered speed and disappeared along the road, heading into the setting sun in the direction of Codgerley. What had she done?

What *had* she done?

In the car, Michael straightened his hat thoughtfully and glanced round at Mrs Considine. She was gazing, unsee-ing, out of the window.

'You did realize she was lying, of course,' he said.

'Yes, Michael,' she replied.

Ahead, the sky had turned to vivid hues of flame and yellow but Mrs Considine spared it not a glance.

At Alison's home, Keith turned on the light at his father's request.

'What did you think of that Mrs Considine?' Mr Allbright asked him.

Keith shrugged.

'She didn't offer to take me to Bransome Park.' He pon-dered for a moment. 'Not that I'd have wanted to go with her anyway. She gave me the creeps.'

He sat down again and picked up his book but he didn't look at it straight away.

'I thought she seemed to be after something,' he said, 'but I can't think what.'

'Neither can I,' said Mr Allbright, looking wryly round the room.

'Anyway,' said Keith, 'whatever it was she didn't get it.' He returned to his book.

Alison, breathing hard, was just slipping in through the back door again. Her thoughts were in turmoil. What *had* she done?

5
A Little Secret

During the next few days, Alison was beset by conflicting emotions.

It was a new experience for her to have to keep a guilty secret from her parents, and she hated it. She cheered herself up to some extent by deciding that after she had been to Bransome Park with Mrs Considine she would confess what she had done. She knew that there would be big trouble, but anything would be better than having to keep it secret for ever more. She just couldn't do that.

At the same time she was kept in a state of tremulous excitement by actually having something to look forward to. To be travelling to Bransome Park in a Rolls-Royce next Saturday when she hadn't even been expecting to go in the school coach!

She longed to drop the information casually at school during lunch, but the fear that it might reach Keith's ears, though unlikely, prevented her. On the Thursday, however, when the subject came up, she couldn't resist a hint. Jenny Allingham was talking about the outing when she glanced across at Alison and said: 'Of course – you're not going, are you?'

Rather than simply say 'no', Alison said primly: 'Not on the *school's* outing, no.'

'Going in the Rolls-Royce, are you?' grinned Stephen Kirkpatrick, totally flooring her. Luckily someone else was speaking at the time so she was able to lapse into her usual silence without any further questioning. She decided that her triumph would come when she revealed herself to them at Bransome Park on Saturday in the company of her friend, Mrs Considine, perhaps stepping out of the Rolls-Royce. Since she'd be confessing to her parents afterwards, that would be all right.

Especially would she want Raine to see her; Susannah Strickland, too, but above all, Raine. She day-dreamed about that during lessons. She hadn't spoken to Raine all week.

Lunch was at one o'clock on Saturday and as soon as it was over she went up to her room and changed into her best dress. She didn't like it very much because it made her look long and skinny – her mother had picked it up in some sale and it didn't really fit her – but the only alternatives were her school clothes or jeans and neither appealed to her, not for an occasion like this. Then she went downstairs and called through the partly-open living room door: 'Going out for a long walk, Mum. See you when I see you.'

Almost without pausing she opened the front door and left the house. She could hear her mother calling from the scullery in reply, something like, 'Right you are, love,' and then something else which she didn't catch because she was too anxious to get out in case anybody saw her and realized that she was hardly likely to be going for a long walk dressed like that. She knew that Keith had gone to his bedroom and her father was out in the back garden, but they might put in an appearance.

Anyway, it didn't matter what her mother said. It wouldn't be anything important.

She felt like an escaping convict as she walked quickly down the front path, alert and fearful in case any of the warders spotted her, a tingling feeling of wanting to bolt for it, but restraining herself for fear of attracting attention.

Once outside the gate, however, she couldn't resist it. Ahead, an afternoon of thrilling freedom beckoned. But as long as she was within hailing distance of the house she was in danger of being called back, maybe to do a job or something like that. She broke into a run. She was filled with a feeling of exhilaration, the sort of feeling she'd almost forgotten was possible.

She had just reached the bend in Holtwood Lane when her mother arrived at the gate, calling her name ineffectually. Mrs Allbright was in time to catch a glimpse of her before she disappeared. She called once more but Alison had gone.

There was a worried expression on Mrs Allbright's face as she went back into the house. Her husband was coming into the living room from the back garden. 'Something the matter?' he asked.

'Alison's just gone out. She said she was going for a walk and I wanted to ask her to get some cough sweets if she passed the chemist's. But when I went after her she was running off and she was wearing her best dress.'

'Best dress! For a walk?' Mr Allbright was puzzled. 'She never wears that anyway, does she –' He looked at his wife suddenly. 'You don't think . . .'

'She couldn't be going with that woman, could she?' said Mrs Allbright. But she didn't sound very sure.

'I'm going to see if there's any sign of her,' said her husband.

He walked stiffly down the lane. As he came out from under the railway bridge he saw a dark blue Rolls-Royce pass along the main road in front of him, heading towards the town. He increased his pace but when he reached the main road there was no sign of the car or Alison. He knew it was too much of a coincidence, though.

'I've a good mind to tell the police,' he said angrily when he got back home. 'Who is that woman, anyway? How did she and Alison fix it up?'

Mrs Allbright dissuaded him from going to the police. They would look silly, she thought. After all, it was almost certain that they were worrying over nothing. It was hardly likely that Mrs Considine was anything other than the thoroughly respectable, wealthy society lady that she seemed to be. It would be Alison who was to blame for this. She had managed to find Mrs Considine again and tell her some lie. No, there wasn't really any danger. It was just the principle, that was all.

'Yes, it is the principle,' said Mr Allbright, grimly. 'All right, all right, but just wait till Alison gets back.'

Alison was in the Rolls-Royce, sitting shyly beside Mrs

Considine and eating chocolates which had been offered to her from a box which lay on the seat between them.

She had been a little apprehensive that it was all too good to be true and that when it came to it, Mrs Considine wouldn't turn up. But the Rolls had overtaken her before she had even got to the Post Office. It had slid to a stop beside her and the chauffeur had sprung out, not in the casual sort of way in which he acted on the two previous occasions that she had met him, but very smartly. He had opened the rear door for her and stood rigidly to attention while she got in, welcomed by Mrs Considine's sideways smile and helping hand. She guessed that Mrs Considine had ordered him to be specially smart today for her benefit, so that she would feel really special on her outing.

And she did feel special, sitting there watching Sturridge slide by. She hoped desperately that she would see someone she knew from school and that they would see her, but there was no sign of anybody. Of course, the people in her form would be on the coach to Bransome Park by now. They'd be somewhere on the road ahead. Perhaps they'd pass them!

Alison had so often imagined herself in situations like this that it was quite hard to convince herself that it wasn't simply another day-dream. What a pulse of excitement it gave her to be able to reassure herself that this was real, this was happening!

It occurred to her for the first time how much Mrs Considine resembled the pretend mother that she sometimes guiltily dreamed about. How easy now to slip into a little day-dream that this really was her mother beside her, that her name was Alison Considine (nice to be able to give this other self of hers a name at last!) and that this was the way she always lived.

Mrs Considine was offering her another chocolate. How amazing the whole thing was!

There was something Alison would have liked to discuss with Mrs Considine. She would have liked to have told her about the woman who had watched her from the train and also how she'd had the silly idea that Michael might have run over her bike deliberately. She'd have liked to have seen how Mrs Considine reacted because these thoughts had kept on coming back to her over the past two or three days. However, she was too shy as yet. Perhaps by the end of the afternoon . . .

'You haven't asked me yet,' said Mrs Considine, smiling, 'if I managed to get tickets all right.'

Alison wouldn't have presumed to ask such a question. It would have seemed impertinent.

'Well, I did. They'll be waiting for us,' continued Mrs Considine chattily. 'I didn't think there'd be any difficulty. I was at school with Lady Pownell. I didn't know her very well – she was two forms above me – but I didn't think she'd turn down a heartfelt appeal. We had a very nice chat over the telephone – and I told her how much you wanted to go.'

It took the dumbfounded Alison a little while to absorb that information. So her name had been discussed in high places – with no less a person than Lady Pownell, the lady of Bransome Park.

They were leaving Sturridge behind now, heading south-eastwards towards the motorway. Mrs Considine was continuing to look at her.

'Tell me about yourself,' she said to Alison. 'Tell me, for instance, about your school. Are you happy there?'

No one had ever asked Alison that question before and for a moment she was disconcerted. The easy thing would have been just to say 'Yes' and leave it at that, and with anyone but Mrs Considine she would have done so. Apart from anything else, she had a pride about not wanting anyone to feel sorry for her. Not in a million years, normally, would she ever have admitted that she was lonely, however obvious it must be.

But Mrs Considine was different. Just as Alison hadn't minded her entering the house, she didn't mind being open with her because she herself was so far above the world in which Alison lived.

'No,' said Alison. 'I hate it.'

What a wonderful feeling of relief to be able to say that! 'Why?' said Mrs Considine.

Now that she'd said it, there was no reason why she shouldn't say more. About Raine. And Susannah Strickland. And Stephen Kirkpatrick. About her home and her parents and Keith. She even told Mrs Considine how she had gone to Codgerley to spy and see if they really were having a barbecue. She'd never expected to find herself confessing that sort of thing to anybody, and yet it came out very naturally.

'So you think you're missing out on things, do you?' said Mrs Considine at last. She was gazing thoughtfully out of the window.

Alison didn't reply. 'Missing out' was nowhere near strong enough a term for the emotions she often felt, the feelings of anger and jealousy and sometimes sheer misery. But she believed that Mrs Considine knew that.

She turned her attention to the road. They were just joining the motorway. Alison had only once travelled on a motorway before and this was exciting.

'We have some boats at Rosewilder, don't we, Michael,' said Mrs Considine, rousing herself from whatever she'd been thinking about. 'We have a sailing dinghy and that sort of cabin cruiser thing and – is there something else?'

'Just the canoe, Mrs Considine.'

'Oh, yes, of course.'

'Rosewilder?' said Alison, whose confidence was growing. 'Is that where you live? Your house?'

'Yes. It's by the lake. By Codgerley.'

'Codgerley?' repeated Alison, surprised. She tried to place Rosewilder but couldn't. However, Codgerley was enormous. There must be quite a few houses round it, secreted amongst the woods.

'Of course, I don't use the boats myself,' said Mrs Considine, who was gazing out of the window again. 'Anne goes out in the sailing dinghy a lot, doesn't she, Michael? She's very good at sailing –'

She glanced round at Alison.

'Anne is my housekeeper. She's a charming girl. Anne Housman. She and Michael are married.'

An idea suddenly seemed to occur to her.

'You know, it's an awful pity that the boats aren't used

47

more. Alison, perhaps I can persuade you to come over to Rosewilder sometimes and go out sailing. I'm sure Anne would be delighted to teach you – ' She looked quite excited by the idea. 'Does that appeal to you?'

Alison could hardly believe that she had heard aright. But she had.

'Oh, *yes*,' she said.

'There's the pony, too, if you'd like to learn to ride. And we have a tennis court and a swimming pool. There are all sorts of things at Rosewilder that you'd find fun.'

Mrs Considine saw the expression of delight and wonder that had dawned upon Alison's face and knew that she needed no reply. She looked at the driving mirror. Michael was looking into it, too, and their eyes met momentarily in a look of complicity.

In her excitement, Alison had forgotten that she wasn't even supposed to be out with Mrs Considine.

'Oh, look!' she said suddenly. 'There's the school coach.'

She'd noticed the name 'Simmons of Sturridge Minster' on the royal blue coach they were overtaking and caught a glimpse of heads at the windows. Raine's might be amongst them. Excitedly she started to turn round so that she'd be able to look out of the rear window, to see and be seen.

Only to find that Mrs Considine was placing a restraining hand on her arm.

'Just one thing, Alison. A little whim of mine. I'd rather you weren't seen by anyone you know. Not yet. Let this be our little secret. Only for a while!'

'Oh – all right,' said Alison, momentarily nonplussed and disappointed. She turned and sat straight in her seat again. She couldn't imagine why Mrs Considine should want to keep it secret.

But what did it matter? Everything that was happening as a result of meeting Mrs Considine was so marvellous that she wasn't going to bother her head about a comparatively little thing like that. Soon be at Bransome Park now.

6
At Bransome Park

The concert was terrific. Not just the actual performances, though they were that, but the whole thing. Sitting in the front row, almost at the feet of the performers – Mrs Considine had managed to get the very best seats – with chocolates and ice creams and drinks constantly pressed upon her, alternately shaking with laughter at the comedians and moved by the songs. And all out of doors in a beautiful setting under a warm sun.

Then, afterwards, tea at a table in a garden surrounded by rhododendrons and azaleas.

The pleasure was sharpened by the knowledge that everyone else in the form was also there among the crowds – but watching the performances from the cheaper seats and buying their refreshments from stalls where they had to queue up.

Alison did once catch a glimpse of some of the people from school, Raine and Susannah Strickland and Jenny Allingham among them. She was by herself at the time, standing near the entrance to the garden where they had just had tea. Mrs Considine had asked her to wait for her there while she went over and had a few words with Lady Pownell whom she had spotted in the distance.

Alison was, on the whole, relieved not to be asked to accompany her. To have to make conversation with the lady of Bransome Park, though it might make a memory to treasure and perhaps boast about ('Yes, I did meet Lady Pownell while I was there'), might be a bit too overpowering on top of all the afternoon's other excitements.

Not that Lady Pownell *looked* overpowering. She was a

small woman in a sagging yellow cardigan. Alison watched as Mrs Considine joined her. There was a handshake and some animated conversation, then they strolled away together to be lost to sight for a minute or two behind trees. It was at that point, as Alison was reflecting that Mrs Considine managed to make Lady Pownell appear positively seedy just by being beside her, that Raine and Susannah and Jenny and the others came wandering along from the same direction.

Alison experienced a pang of jealousy as she saw that Raine was laughing at something Susannah Strickland said. Susannah was talking animatedly and everybody, including Raine, appeared to be absorbed by what she was saying . . .

Alison longed to let them see her, but she didn't want to go against Mrs Considine's wishes and she stepped back out of sight instead. Soon afterwards, Mrs Considine returned.

There was a slightly odd moment as she did so. Alison had been looking in a different direction and the first indication she had of Mrs Considine's approach was the sound of her voice. She was calling something which sounded like 'car'. Glancing round, Alison saw that Mrs Considine was looking directly at her.

'Car?' Alison repeated, puzzled. It seemed a funny thing to be calling. 'Do you mean it's time to get back to the car?'

Mrs Considine laughed. 'Yes, that's what I mean,' she said. 'Let's go there now.' But Alison didn't think she had meant that. She couldn't understand it.

Not that she thought about it for very long. As they made their way back to the car park she was simply thinking what a fabulous afternoon it had been. And still was. It wasn't over yet. Michael, who had been left to his own devices for the last three hours or so, was waiting to open the car door for them very smartly and usher them into the cosy and inviting interior.

Alison knew that a lot of people in her form found car journeys very boring, but she didn't. She hadn't had enough of them for that. She loved them. And as they travelled back along the motorway she felt so snug that her only regret was that the journey should ever come to an end and that she would be deposited outside her home again –

Home! And a confession to make.

It was just as that very unpleasant thought struck her that Mrs Considine, who had been silent for some time, turned to her and said idly: 'Alison, what made your parents change their minds so quickly about allowing you to come with me today?'

The direct question coming on top of Alison's own thoughts was a double blow which thoroughly disconcerted her. She blushed.

'I don't really know,' she replied weakly. 'They just did.'

Under Mrs Considine's steady and increasingly suspicious gaze, she became even more confused and embarrassed.

'Alison,' said Mrs Considine, 'you *are* telling me the truth, aren't you? They did change their minds, didn't they?'

Alison didn't need to say anything more. The answer was written all over her face.

'Oh, Alison,' said Mrs Considine, reproachfully, 'you've lied to me, haven't you? Now you really have put me in a most difficult position.'

The utterly woebegone expression on Alison's face seemed to melt her a little. In much kinder tones she said: 'Well, I shall have to sort this out, won't I. I'll come in with you and see your parents when you get back home. But, Alison, you should *not* have done that. And there was I hoping you would be able to come and visit Rosewilder. I *hope* that will still be possible.'

There was a ghost of a smile on Michael's face as, listening, he watched the road ahead.

Alison was dreading the row that she thought was going to come, but in fact it didn't work out like that at all.

The sight of Mrs Considine marching up the path with Alison in tow, then sweeping in and saying how furious she had been when she had found out, but that they mustn't be too angry because it obviously had been such a

51

tremendous temptation, and perhaps she herself was mostly to blame . . . Well, it all completely took the wind out of her parents' sails.

Alison soon realized that they had found out about her lie, anyway. But it was difficult for them to remain angry when it was so obvious that they had been utterly wrong to harbour even the merest suspicion of Mrs Considine.

Of *Mrs Considine*! This wealthy and highly-respected lady who herself expected such high standards of conduct and who moved in the very best circles and was a friend of – of *who*? Of *Lady Pownell*? Lord and Lady Pownell who owned Bransome Park! She had been at *school* with her?

And they, the Allbrights of Number 2, Holtwood Lane, the less than nothings, had forbidden their daughter to go out with her!

Alison, watching their faces, knew what was passing through their minds and that she was safe. Their previous fears seemed silly to them now, not only because she had been out and come back safely, but because she had clearly been severely ticked off for deceiving them by the very person they had warned her against!

Alison's mother warmed further to Mrs Considine when the latter, after asking for and receiving a cup of tea, told them why it was that she had been particularly interested in Alison and had wanted to take her out for a treat. It was a reason which gave Alison a shock, though at first she couldn't think why.

'You obviously,' said Mrs Considine to Mr and Mrs Allbright, 'thought I was a little bit *pushing* about taking Alison out, didn't you?'

'Well, yes, we did really,' admitted Mrs Allbright, guilt-ily.

'The reason for that is quite simple,' said Mrs Considine. 'The fact is that Alison reminds me of my own daughter. They are quite remarkably alike.'

'You have a daughter!' exclaimed Mrs Allbright. 'And she's just like Alison?'

'Yes,' Mrs Considine confirmed. She was smiling but there was something bright about her smile as there had been once before.

'Well, isn't that a coincidence,' said Mrs Allbright. 'Somebody who looks like you, Alison. Mrs Considine must have got a surprise when she first saw you.'

'Yes, I did,' said Mrs Considine.

Alison was analysing why the news had come as such a blow to her. She knew that it was because she was jealous. She had come to feel during the afternoon that there was some sort of special relationship between Mrs Considine and herself. It had been almost as if her day-dream mother had come to life and she had been spending the afternoon with her. She, her daughter.

Now, unexpectedly, she had learned that there was somebody who occupied that role in real life. Some fortunate girl who lived the life that Alison could only dream about. She couldn't help but be jealous.

But that was silly, wasn't it. She must put such emotions aside, be thankful for the good things that seemed to be coming her way at last, stop always wanting more . . .

Mrs Considine was sipping her tea, pensively. She wasn't smiling now.

'Yes,' she said, almost as if speaking to herself, 'my daughter's all I have now. I'm divorced, you see. My husband and I separated a few years ago. I'm afraid we didn't get on.'

Mrs Allbright tutted sympathetically. Alison knew that such sad confidences were just what were required to put her mother right on Mrs Considine's side. Afterwards she would probably say: 'You see, it's not all fun being rich. Rich people aren't usually the happy ones. I wouldn't want to be rich myself.'

'You didn't take your daughter to the concert today, then?' said Mr Allbright, who looked a little puzzled. He was standing by the fireplace, supporting himself with one elbow on the mantelpiece.

Keith, who was sitting in the corner and not saying a word, was staring at Mrs Considine.

'She's at school in Switzerland,' she said. 'I feel I have to do what's best for her, though of course I miss her terribly.'

'You must do,' nodded Mrs Allbright who, as Alison was well aware, was capable of heartfelt sympathy for the most privileged and undeserving of people if their supposed hard luck was put to her in the right way.

Mrs Considine had been accepted as being all right by both Alison's mother and her father. And when she left soon afterwards, it had somehow been agreed that Alison could come and visit her on the following Saturday and go out sailing with Anne Housman, and maybe ride the pony too and learn to play tennis or anything else that might take her fancy while she was there.

There was even a suggestion that such visits might become a regular weekend occurrence. And that when Mrs Considine's own daughter arrived home for the school holidays she and Alison might become friends . . .

Alison went outside with her parents to see her off and to say goodbye to Michael. She had managed to push the jealousy out of her mind and was full of excitement at the prospect that lay before her. At last something good had happened. Her parents seemed happy, too, impressed and awed that Alison had made a rich and influential friend.

Mrs Considine lowered the car window a little to speak privately to Alison before being driven away. 'You will remember this is our secret for the time being, won't you?' she smiled. 'What about your brother – is he discreet?'

'Oh, Keith won't say anything,' replied Alison.

She waved till the car turned out of sight round the bend.

Her parents paused for a moment to enjoy the evening air so that Alison was first back in the house. Keith was still sitting in the corner.

'Did you believe all that stuff about her having a daughter like you?' he said.

'What do you mean, did I believe it?' said Alison. 'Of course I believe it.'

'Then why didn't she say anything about it when she was here before? Surely she would have done if it's really true.'

'Oh, you get on my nerves,' said Alison. 'As if she'd tell a lie about it! You're just jealous because nothing nice ever happens to you and nothing ever will unless you make it. You're just trying to spoil things for me, but you won't – '

'Stop quarrelling!' shouted her father as he came in through the door. 'I'm sick of hearing you two fighting.'

' – not all fun being rich,' her mother was saying as she closed the door behind her. 'Rich people aren't always happy. I can do without being rich myself.'

Alison had already dismissed Keith's words from her mind. She was more interested in recalling that she had forgotten to mention to Mrs Considine the business of the woman who had stared at her from the train. Because if Mrs Considine had a daughter who resembled Alison, that could have been the reason for her interest, couldn't it?

Still, she would definitely mention it next weekend.

If Keith had caused Alison to doubt the existence of Mrs Considine's daughter – which he hadn't because it would have been ridiculous to do so – her doubts would soon have been dispelled anyway. She heard more about the daughter at, of all unlikely places, the school dinner table on Monday.

The conversation had turned, inevitably, to the concert at Bransome Park which everyone agreed had been very good. Alison just kept quiet, listening. Jenny Allingham was talking.

'Did any of you see Lady Pownell?' she was saying.

'Wouldn't recognize her if I did,' said Paul Longstaff.

'Susannah pointed her out to us,' said Jenny. 'She met her once with her parents at some do.'

'Trust Susannah!' thought Alison, her eyes on her meat loaf and mashed potatoes.

'She was with another woman that Susannah recognized,' continued Jenny, 'somebody called Mrs Considine.'

Alison was suddenly alert. She was remembering seeing Jenny and Susannah and Raine at Bransome Park. Susannah had been telling the others something then; they'd been laughing about it . . .

'Susannah saw her at some do last year as well. Why she remembered her was because she had her daughter with her and this girl looked exactly like somebody we know.'

Alison glanced up to see that Jenny was gazing at her.

'You mean Breezy?' asked Stephen Kirkpatrick with a gurgling laugh.

'That's right. Susannah said this girl was so like Alison she couldn't believe it.'

So that's what they'd been talking about!

'Poor girl!' grinned Stephen Kirkpatrick.

'It seems she looked exactly like her, but' (Alison found that 'but' still more unflattering than what Stephen had said) 'at the same time she looked very attractive, glamorous in fact.'

'That,' said Stephen Kirkpatrick, grinning yet more widely, 'sounds like the most impossible feat of magic ever performed.'

The conversation moved on. Alison was scarlet. But she wasn't thinking so much of her own confusion, wasn't even bothering to feel resentful of the way they had discussed her as if she weren't there. This second mention of Mrs Considine's daughter had given her a strange, if foolish, feeling.

It was as if there were another Alison Allbright in existence. Some shadowy figure, some other self who led the life and had the things that she, the first Alison Allbright, only day-dreamed about.

As if, in fact, her day-dreams had come to life. Yes, it was a very silly thought but it did make her feel peculiar. A really funny feeling.

7
Rosewilder

On the following Saturday Alison, carrying a plastic carrier bag, travelled to Rosewilder in the Rolls-Royce. She was picked up by Michael at the corner of Holtwood Lane immediately after lunch.

She took careful note of how to get there because on future occasions – supposing there were any – she might be going on her new bike. After driving about three miles down the Ardington Road towards Codgerley Lake, they forked right into quite a narrow little road which twisted and turned through woods and low green hills, gently climbing all the time until at last they broke from amongst some trees and Alison saw that Codgerley was to their left and a little below them. She realized that they were on top of those wooded slopes which could be seen in the distance from the spot where the barbecue had been held.

The car plunged into woods again before slowing to turn left at a signpost which said simply 'Rosewilder'. They glided, in almost perfect silence it seemed, down an even narrower little road which descended towards the lake shore. Down beneath an archway of overhanging trees till they passed through big open wooden gates set in a high wall and came to a stop on the wide expanse of paving stones in front of a long, pale, gracious house with elegant windows and a terrace.

Beyond a low stone wall which enclosed the paved area, Alison could see the lake between trees. Some broad, shallow steps led down towards it. There were several statues and an ornate fountain, and the whole place had a rather exotic feel about it. She could easily have believed that the expanse of water was the Mediterranean, rather than Codgerley. It all made Holtwood Lodge look nothing.

Michael opened the car door for her, standing to attention as he did so. At the same time, Mrs Considine emerged from the house, descending the steps from the front door. She was smiling that sideways smile of hers. Alison realized, to her surprise, that she must have been looking out for her arrival. Behind Mrs Considine came a young woman in a dark dress. She was pretty, demure-looking with dark hair and eyes, rosy cheeks and full lips.

'There,' Mrs Considine said to her, 'didn't I tell you she's just like Camilla?'

Camilla! So that was the name of Mrs Considine's daughter.

To Alison, who was now standing awkwardly by the car, holding the plastic carrier bag, Mrs Considine said: 'This is Anne, my housekeeper. She's going to take you out sailing and anything else you'd like to do. She's terribly good at everything. So good that I can't understand how I can keep her working for me.'

Anne, who was gazing at Alison as if mesmerized by her, smiled. 'If I have learned to be good at things it's only because I've had the chance through working for you, Mrs Considine.' Then she inclined her head to Alison and said deferentially: 'Pleased to meet you.'

She was showing more deference to Alison than to Mrs Considine. Alison found it embarrassing – but it was a little bit flattering, too. She'd never met a private maidservant before and that, she supposed, was what Anne really was.

'Let's get you kitted out first, shall we,' said Mrs Considine, running her eyes over Alison's clothes. Alison hadn't known quite what to do about clothes so she had come in her best dress, in order to look as smart as she could manage, while in her carrier bag she was carrying her jeans and jumper, which she intended to use for sailing or anything else requiring casual wear.

Mrs Considine wasn't very impressed by them, however, when Alison showed them to her.

'No, no. I think we can do better than that,' she said. 'I've laid a few things out for you.'

She led the way up the steps and into the house and Alison followed her rather nervously.

She was nervous because she wasn't sure how to behave in a house like this. Her knowledge of the residences of the rich came almost entirely from books, most of them out-of-date. In these books, the houses frequently had morning rooms and drawing rooms and breakfast rooms, each of which had a different purpose which was apparently well known to the occupants and their guests, who were always in the right one at the right time. Also, conversation always seemed rather stilted and formal, with servants appearing discreetly from time to time and then withdrawing.

Alison walked as quietly as she could along the long, carpeted corridor.

'I laid them on a chair in the drawing room,' said Mrs Considine. 'Along here.'

The drawing room was graceful and airy with french windows overlooking the lake. Alison took in the pale walls and salmon coloured curtains, the expensive Eastern carpets on the polished wood floor, the elegant furniture. It was considerably bigger than the whole of the ground floor of 2, Holtwood Lane.

'Here you are,' said Mrs Considine, 'you can change in the bathroom.'

Draped over the arm of a chair were various articles of clothing, among them some shorts, a sailing anorak, a thin sweater, a life-jacket, riding breeches, riding hat . . . A pair of sailing shoes was lying by the chair.

Alison stared.

'Are these – ?' she began.

'Camilla's. I'm sure they'll all fit you. You're just her size.'

'But . . . but won't she mind?'

'No, she won't mind,' said Mrs Considine rather abruptly. 'In fact when you come here I'd like you to look upon these things exactly as if they're your own. Afterwards, I'll show you where they're normally kept. Now, if you'd like to put the sailing things on in the bathroom you can leave the rest there for the time being till you need them.'

A few minutes later, Alison stood gazing at herself in the full-length mirror in the downstairs bathroom. She was wearing the shorts, the light sweater, anorak and the sailing shoes. It was funny how such simple things made her look and feel different. She was in the habit of wearing rather dowdy cast-offs which her mother picked up for her in various places, whereas Camilla Considine's clothes, though simple and casual, were in fact expensive and well-made and, even more to the point, had a sort of dash and glamour about them. They made her want to pull her shoulders back and try to move gracefully. They reinforced her feeling that underneath the boring, drippy exterior which she normally presented to the world, there was another, different, exciting Alison Allbright waiting to get out. She could be dashing and glamorous, too . . .

If she had been born Camilla Considine it would have come out right from the beginning. Camilla Considine had simply been lucky enough to be born in the right house.

Anyway, thought Alison as she opened the bathroom door, she knew now that Camilla Considine really did exist. She must do because these were her clothes and her life-jacket.

Then it struck Alison that even to be thinking that must mean that she had, after all, had doubts. But why? Mrs Considine had told her she had a daughter and it had been confirmed by what Jenny Allingham had said. It was as simple as that. Yet, somewhere in the back of her mind, she hadn't quite accepted it. Jealousy, probably.

Mrs Considine was standing in the corridor. She looked Alison up and down as she emerged.

'Even the hair's the same colour,' she said. 'Come here a moment.'

Alison stepped nearer and Mrs Considine moved behind her. She felt the bands that held her bunches being removed and her hair patted into place.

Mrs Considine turned her round to look at her.

'I really must,' she said, 'take you to a decent hairdresser and have it put into some sort of shape. It could be very nice. Now off you go and enjoy yourself.'

Feeling overwhelmed by it all, Alison was led through a

door at the side of the house into a courtyard where Anne, now dressed for sailing, was waiting for her.

As the two of them walked away, turning down the shallow steps that led to the lake shore, Mrs Considine continued to watch Alison. There was no semblance of a smile on her face now.

It was like a veritable sailing club down by the lake shore, thought Alison. A small cabin cruiser was moored at the end of a wooden jetty. Beside it was a sailing dinghy with the mast up, only needing the sails hoisted to be ready to go. Lying on the floor of a wooden shed with an open up-and-over door was a canoe.

All there, presumably, for the pleasure of Camilla Considine when she came home for the holidays.

While Anne got into the sailing dinghy and started hoisting the mainsail, Alison gazed across the lake at the distant shore. She could see some sails out there.

'Are you looking at something special?' Anne asked her, smiling but still with that slightly disconcerting deference.

'I was just wondering if I knew anybody in those boats across there,' said Alison.

'There are some binoculars in the boathouse. I'll get them for you. Then you'll be able to have a proper look.'

Anne got out of the boat, went into the shed and emerged with a pair of binoculars which she handed to Alison.

Alison put them to her eyes and focused them gingerly. She'd never used binoculars before.

Yes! That was the Lees' boat! She still couldn't make out the people all that distinctly, but she was sure that was Kate Lee and her brother Brian . . .

Anybody else?

Raine! Yes, it *was* Raine . . . she was in the Woodwards' boat with Janet Lockwood and Alastair Woodward. Well, at least Susannah Strickland wasn't with her. That was *something*.

'Somebody you know?' Anne asked her as she handed the binoculars back. She nodded. It was very curious to be looking at them from this side of the lake. They'd never have guessed it in a thousand years.

'Do boats ever come across to this side of the lake?' she asked Anne.

'Not very often. The lake's very shallow in the middle and not many people know the channels.'

'But there are channels?'

'Oh yes.'

Perhaps one day, if Mrs Considine didn't tire of her, she would sail out among them, handling her boat beautifully. That would take the wind out of their sails, wouldn't it? Joke!

Once she got into the boat, that day seemed a long way off. She didn't know a reach from a luff or a tack from a run. And she didn't feel she was making a very brilliant pupil. It was fun, though, and Anne was very good-humoured and patient *and* deferential even when she did the silliest things, even when she almost turned the boat over! At last, at long last, she was starting to learn to live, to do the sort of things other people did.

This whole thing was so unbelievable! How long could her luck last? She had nothing to offer Mrs Considine in return for what, astonishingly, Mrs Considine was offering her. Absolutely nothing except, apparently, her appearance. How long before Mrs Considine tired of that?

After the sailing, Alison had a cup of tea in the enormous kitchen with Anne. Then she changed into Camilla's riding gear and was taken outside to be introduced to Pippin, the pony, and have her first ride on him in the paddock that lay beyond the gardens. She'd never sat on a pony before, even though she'd always lived in the country, and she was just as clueless at riding as she was at sailing, but Anne remained unfailingly helpful and patient. Alison realized that they were laughing quite a lot. Her shyness and clumsiness had evaporated in the excitement and fun of doing things. She was also glowing and feeling healthily tired. It was quite a shock suddenly to see Anne looking at her watch and saying that it was half past six and she must thing about preparing dinner.

It was just after that, as they were heading back towards

the shed, that there were just a few moments of awkward-
ness. Alison had been wanting to question Anne about
Camilla all afternoon and she now felt that a sufficient
degree of intimacy had been reached for her to be able to
do so. 'What's Camilla like?' she asked. 'Are you and she
friendly?'

But Anne didn't reply. She was leading Pippin while
Alison rode him and she kept on looking straight ahead. It
was as if she hadn't heard, but Alison was sure she had.

Alison was embarrassed, wondering if she'd made some
terrible gaffe by questioning a servant about her mistress.
Then she was distracted by seeing Mrs Considine
approaching from the garden.

'Enjoy yourself this afternoon?' asked Mrs Considine.

Alison nodded eagerly, reining in Pippin. 'You bet – '
she began, then changed it to a more dignified: 'Very
much, thank you.'

Mrs Considine smiled. 'It seems to have done you a lot of
good – doesn't it, Anne? Look at the colour in her cheeks.'

'Yes, you do look very much better than when you
arrived,' Anne said, still in that friendly-deferential way.

Perhaps, thought Alison, she really hadn't heard after
all. Perhaps she'd been in a dream.

'Now you'll be staying to dinner,' said Mrs Considine
practically. 'Would you like to help Anne put Pippin away?
Then after you've had a shower, come and see me and I'll
find you something nice to wear. I like to dress properly
for dinner. I'll be in the kitchen.'

So the day wasn't over yet! Alison had thought she might
be offered something to eat and had urged her mother not
to save anything, but 'staying to dinner' sounded very grand
and inviting. And she wasn't averse to trying on some
more of Camilla Considine's clothes. It was fun.

It was still early May and there was quite a nip in the air
as, guided by Anne, she took Pippin's saddle off and put
him away in his stable. But that, together with her slightly
aching muscles, simply increased her pleasurable antici-
pation of hot water, nice clothes and a meal. As they
walked back towards the house she was able to look across
Codgerley. There were no sails out on the lake any longer.

It was still and romantic. She could very easily fall in love with Rosewilder.

Five minutes later Alison was under the shower. She felt like singing. As she spread her arms luxuriously into the warm, steaming rain and inhaled the perfume from the expensive soap, she was mentally comparing this sumptuous, green-tiled shower room with the bathroom at home. That had a white enamel bath on claw feet surmounted by a thumping gas geyser, past which you had to edge your way to the tiny sink. It had an uninviting, almost *repelling* atmosphere, as if a bath were a duty you were expected to get over and done with quickly. When she'd grumbled about it once, her father had curtly told her that plenty of people didn't have a bathroom at all.

That might be true, but it didn't alter the facts. If she'd experienced Mrs Considine's shower room she'd have grumbled about it even more.

Mrs Considine had left a dressing gown for her in the shower room and she put it on instead of her dress. Then she set off along the carpeted corridor in the direction of the kitchen. The light was starting to fade outside now.

Before coming to the kitchen she passed an open door. Glancing inside she saw that it was the dining room. Her first impression was of how deliciously romantic it looked, like having a super little restaurant all to yourself, with silver cutlery and a bowl of flowers on a polished oval table. Then she saw that Michael and Anne were in there, standing in the shadows at the other end of the table and looking back at her almost guiltily.

Alison sensed that they had been talking about her while laying the table. Well, why shouldn't they?

'Ah, there you are!' said Mrs Considine, emerging smiling from the kitchen. 'Everything can look after itself for a few minutes now. I like cooking, when Anne will let me. This way.'

She led Alison to the front hall, up the wide curving staircase to the first floor, along a corridor, then opened a door and ushered Alison inside. It was a large, very feminine bedroom.

'There are plenty of clothes in here,' said Mrs Considine,

making for a huge built-in wardrobe which stretched half the length of the room.

'This is your daughter's bedroom, isn't it?' said Alison, still standing just inside the room.

'That's right,' said Mrs Considine, sliding the wardrobe door across. She glanced round, watching Alison.

Alison was staring at a framed portrait on the dressing table. It was of a girl. It was very strange. The face looked just like her own except that, unlike hers, no one could have accused it of appearing 'morose' or 'shrinking'. Though unsmiling, it was the confident face of someone who had been born to the best of everything. It was the face that Alison wanted to see when she looked in the mirror, the face that she'd tried deliberately to cultivate without succeeding.

She knew now what Susannah Strickland had meant when she had said that Camilla Considine was just like Alison *but* very attractive, 'glamorous in fact'.

'And – and that's your daughter,' said Alison.

'Yes,' said Mrs Considine. 'Didn't I tell you that you and she are very much alike? Amazing, isn't it.'

Alison felt a stab of bitter jealousy towards that confident face. That girl was her rival – but a rival who couldn't be beaten. Then she looked at the open wardrobe. For someone as clothes-starved as Alison it was a breathtaking sight.

'Choose something nice to wear for dinner . . .' said Mrs Considine, flicking her way along the row of dresses. 'What about this?'

Like a superior shop assistant she unhooked a dark green velvet dress and displayed it to Alison.

'It's beautiful,' said Alison – and it was. So beautiful that she impulsively moved forward, wanting just to touch it. Then she stopped. There was something wrong about all this. Seeing that array of clothes brought it home to her.

'I can't wear all your daughter's clothes just like this, Mrs Considine,' she said. 'Anyway, I've got my own dress – '

'But Camilla would like you to wear it,' said Mrs Considine. 'She has so many. I don't suppose she'll ever wear this one again herself.'

She was taking the dress off the hanger and spreading it

out on the bed as she spoke, handling it very gently and lovingly. Having done so, she glanced at Alison's puzzled face.

'Surely you'd like that, wouldn't you?' she coaxed. 'When you come here I'd like you to put on Camilla's things and treat her wardrobe exactly like your own. You can put your own things on again when you leave. Wouldn't you find that fun?'

Alison was silent. Of course it would be fun but . . .

Mrs Considine moved towards the door.

'I'll leave you to get dressed then, while I go and see how dinner's getting on. You've got about twenty minutes, car.'

Car? At least, that's what Alison thought she'd said. Like at the concert. What did she mean – car?

It flashed into Alison's mind at the same moment as Mrs Considine put her hand to her forehead and laughed. Not 'car' – just 'Ca'. Short for Camilla!

'I'm calling you "Ca" again,' said Mrs Considine, still laughing. 'That's what I always call my daughter. I'm bound to do that because you're so like her. You don't mind if I call you "Ca" while you're here, do you?'

'But – ' began Alison. Then she stopped because there didn't seem any point in going on.

It was quite clear now that Mrs Considine was playing a game with her. She was encouraging her to play the role of being her daughter, Camilla, to wear her clothes and be called by her name. Why she was doing so Alison didn't understand. Presumably because she was missing her daughter badly and wanted to be reminded of her, though to go to such lengths seemed a bit ridiculous . . .

But she wasn't just *encouraging* Alison. She was *insisting*. It was written in the look on her face. She was smiling but the smile said: 'Do this if you want to come to Rosewilder again.'

Out loud she said: 'Come downstairs for dinner in about twenty minutes' time. I hope you'll be wearing the dress.' She went out and closed the door behind her.

Alison sat down on the bed. She felt that she had been given an ultimatum. If she went downstairs wearing the dress and ready for dinner, it would show that she agreed to Mrs Considine's terms. If she didn't . . .

It was odd. There'd been something odd about this business ever since Michael had run over her bicycle, hadn't there? Would it not be better to go downstairs and ask to be taken home now?

Home! The very thought made Alison shudder. So Mrs Considine was playing a little game! What about it? The longer she played such games the better, as far as Alison was concerned. It was glorious. Suddenly her whole life was changing for the better.

Some fifteen minutes later Mrs Considine was passing through the hall when she saw Alison descending the stairs. Alison was wearing the green dress.

'You look splendid!' she exclaimed. 'Absolutely splendid! And your timing is impeccable. I hope you're hungry, Ca.'

Alison smiled and nodded.

8
An Invitation to Italy

It was extraordinary to be sitting there feeling as if she were somebody else.

Alison was seated on one side of the gleaming dining table, facing Mrs Considine. The candles, in their silver candlesticks, had been lit, causing the room to glow softly. The rose-coloured curtains were drawn back and through the big window to her right, with its low, broad, polished wood sill, she could see Codgerley reflecting the red sunset.

Anne moved quietly about, waiting on them. The meal was not some obscure, unrecognizable dish, as Alison had feared it might be. It was really only mutton with some very superior chips and vegetables, but it was delicious. She had had some difficulty sorting out the chips and vegetables from their separate dishes because at home they just had everything on the one plate, but Anne had come to her aid.

And here she was pretending she was Ca Considine. Since she had decided to go along with Mrs Considine's little games she might as well make the most of it, might as well revel in it.

Ca Considine! How upper class it sounded! Almost ridiculously so! What fun to be called that! What fun if she could go round school calling herself Ca Considine!

But there was something she wanted to ask. She was trying to pluck up the courage to do so.

'Nice?' Mrs Considine was inquiring, referring to the meal.

'Mmmm,' said Alison. 'It's absolutely marvellous.' She

68

hesitated. Courage came. 'Mrs Considine . . . did you ever happen to go past our house on a train – it'd be about a fortnight ago now?'

'I've been wondering when you were going to ask me that,' said Mrs Considine. She poured herself a glass of water, drank from it and put it down. Amused, she looked at Alison again. 'You should now ask me whether I asked Michael to run over your bicycle.'

Astounded, Alison stared at her.

'Then you – you – '

'I saw you from the train, was struck by how like my daughter you were, and decided that I wanted to get to know you.'

Mrs Considine placed one of the superior chips in her mouth and watched Alison as if studying her reaction. She, Mrs Considine, still looked amused.

'But – ' began Alison. She paused.

'Destroying your bicycle was rather a liberty? Yes, it was, wasn't it? But I felt I wanted to do things for a girl who is so like my daughter. So I had to have some excuse. I had to do something to get the relationship off on the right footing. You're not annoyed with me, are you?'

This last was said with a mock-anxious pout of her lips. Alison, conscious of her surroundings, of the meal, of the healthy glow she felt from her activities of the afternoon, of the splendid new bicycle that was now hers, grinned and shook her head.

'Good,' said Mrs Considine with a large mock sigh of relief. 'Then let us talk of other things such as whether you like custard with your pudding. *I* do.'

The subject was apparently disposed of. Alison would have liked to pursue it further, but she wasn't to be allowed to. But what did it matter? It seemed more important that she was becoming steadily more easy in Mrs Considine's company. It had always taken her ages to come out of her shell with anyone new, but Mrs Considine had the knack of putting her at her ease. It was the clothes, too. To be dressed so well made her feel more alive and animated than she usually did.

Over the pudding, Mrs Considine became rather abstracted, gazing absently out of the window. Then suddenly she said, 'Have you felt today that you haven't been missing out quite so much as you usually do?'

'Oh, today's been . . . oh . . . I can't describe it.'

'How else do you feel you're missing out? Tell me what it is you really want.'

Alison considered. 'I'd just like to do everything everybody else does – and more. I'd like to be able to do all sorts of things: travel a lot; go to lots of different countries; wear nice clothes.'

Mrs Considine was still looking out of the window. 'Do you not think,' she said, 'that perhaps that's all rather shallow? Is there nothing more you want than that?'

Alison looked at her uneasily. There had been a note of sharpness in Mrs Considine's voice. It was a little disconcerting. Alison couldn't see the expression on her face, which was in shadow. Was she annoyed?

'Well, I dunno,' said Alison, defensively. 'Is it? I suppose if you've got the money to do all these things and always have done them, then it's easy to say it's shallow. But if you haven't – '

She suddenly realized that Mrs Considine had turned her head and was looking at her again. She didn't seem annoyed now. She looked amused.

'Oh, I'm sorry,' said Alison, flustered. 'I didn't mean you personally. I meant – '

'I know,' said Mrs Considine, soothingly. 'Anyway, I'm glad you've found today worthwhile. You must come here next Saturday and – let me see – yes – the Saturday after . . .'

Alison's heart leapt. This was just what she wanted to hear.

' – but I shall be going to Italy for a week on the Saturday after that.'

Alison felt disappointed.

'That's half-term week,' she said. She always found that, even though she didn't like school and in theory longed for the holidays, when they actually arrived they dragged horribly. It would have been marvellous to have had Rosewilder to look forward to.

'Your half-term?' Mrs Considine sounded interested. 'How long do you get?'

'Well, the Monday – that's the bank holiday – and then all the rest of the week.'

'That sounds most convenient,' said Mrs Considine. She pushed her plate aside and folded her arms on the table in front of her. 'Just the week I'm going. Why don't you come with me? You said that travelling was one of the things you really want to do.'

Alison stared at her. After a few moments Mrs Considine spread her hands in a helpless gesture.

'You seem to have been struck dumb,' she said. 'Would you like to come or wouldn't you?'

'I don't know whether you're joking or not,' said Alison in a small voice.

'Of course I'm not joking. I go every year to a small hotel on the coast. I should be delighted to have your company. Do you have a passport?'

'No,' said Alison. A wave of excitement was starting to work its way methodically through her, starting in her head and tingling its way downwards. 'Do you mean it? Do you really mean it?'

'I'll need your parents' permission and they'll have to get a passport for you,' said Mrs Considine, comfortably. 'But I think that'll be all right. I think they've realized by now that I'm quite harmless.'

Alison had a sudden thought. 'But what about your daughter? Won't you be seeing her at half-term?'

'No,' said Mrs Considine. 'Her half-term is at a different time.'

The excitement couldn't be contained any longer.

'Oh, Mrs Considine, I'm bursting to tell people. *Can't* I tell anybody?'

'Not yet. Let's keep this a secret from everybody except your family just a little while longer – maybe until you come back from Italy. And, Ca – '

'Yes?'

'I wouldn't even tell your family about the game we play. It's just a whim of mine.'

'I won't.'

Alison wouldn't do anything to upset Mrs Considine now. *Not anything*!

'Incidentally – your brother, Keith. Are you sure he won't say anything about me to his friends at school?'

'Keith doesn't have any friends,' said Alison, contemptuously. 'He doesn't talk to anybody, either. Keith's a non-person.'

Anne was coming in through the door with a tray.

'Your coffee, Miss Camilla,' she said.

Travelling home in the car, Alison sat with her eyes closed. She was day-dreaming. But it was a new day-dream. The old one was now out-of-date. She had modernized it.

In this day-dream she was Camilla (Ca to her family and friends) Considine, address: Rosewilder, Sturridge Minster. She was on holiday from her school in Switzerland – no, she wasn't, that was too much of a strain on the imagination – on second thoughts, she was being educated privately, at home at Rosewilder – and she was on her way to visit some people called Allbright. They were nice people, Mr and Mrs Allbright and their son Keith, and she was going to see if she could bring a little brightness into their lives. Maybe she'd be able to give them a few things, take them for an outing in the Rolls because they didn't have a car of their own. They led very drab lives.

This day-dream was very much easier to sustain and believe in than any she had ever had before, because for several hours she had been living the life of Ca Considine.

After she had got out of the car at the corner of Holtwood Lane and waved goodbye to Michael she ought to have snapped out of her day-dream. But she didn't. She still felt more like Ca Considine than Alison Allbright. It was as if she were hovering between the two personalities and in some ways, Ca Considine was the more real to her. Holtwood Lodge, when she passed it, appeared quite small and rather shabby.

As she entered the living room at home, however, she was brought down to earth very rapidly. Her mother was seated by the table watching television. She was much too close to the set for comfort and she had the sound turned down low. The reason for this was that Alison's father was stretched out on the floor fast asleep, a cushion at his head for a pillow. This reduced the already small amount of usable floor space to virtually nothing and, rather than step over him to get to the other side of the table, Mrs Allbright was putting up with sitting almost on top of the television set.

Alison's father had a habit of doing this, much to her mortification. He complained of having difficulty in keeping his eyes open in the evening when it was still too early to go to bed, so he would simply lie down on the floor. It definitely lowered the tone of the place.

Keith wasn't there. He had presumably gone to bed.

'Alison!' exclaimed her mother, rising to her feet. 'Did you have a nice time? I've saved you some supper, I've been keeping it warm.'

'Oh, Mum, I told you not to. You said you wouldn't –'

'I thought I ought to be on the safe side. You can eat it, can't you?'

The very thought was nauseating.

She was Alison Allbright again. It was horrible.

'Italy?' said her father disbelievingly at breakfast next morning when Alison had summoned up the courage to ask him.

'*Italy*?' repeated her mother.

'That's right,' said Alison. 'Italy.'

Keith munched his toast and stared.

'I don't follow,' said Mr Allbright. 'Is she expecting us to pay for you going to Italy with her because – '

'Oh no, Dad, no. That never even came up. *She'd* be paying.' Alison didn't know how she was going to be able to live through the next few minutes of unbearable suspense. She couldn't really guess how they'd take it. The Allbright household had never before been confronted by a situation like this, so there were no precedents, no guide-lines.

Mrs Allbright shook her head in wonder. 'She's got more money than she knows what to do with,' she said. 'Doesn't know what to chuck it away on next.'

Alison liked the sound of those words. They indicated tolerance, a readiness to accept the situation. She looked at her father. He was gazing at his plate and pulling his mouth into funny shapes, no doubt groping for reasons why she shouldn't go.

'Why's she want to take you with her?' he said. 'Why not her own daughter?' Before Alison could reply he answered his own question, grudgingly. 'Oh, she's at some school abroad, isn't she?'

'Yes,' said Alison.

'I feel sorry for her,' said Mrs Allbright. 'Living alone in that great house, miles from anywhere. Just some servants to wait on her hand and foot. Nobody to think about but herself! I wouldn't like to be her and if she wants to cheer herself up by having Alison for company, then let Alison have the benefit of it.'

'Oh, thank you, Mum, thank you,' thought Alison, turning pleading eyes on her father. One down, one to go.

He looked as if he still wanted to object but was weakening under the pressure of female domination. He started to say something, hesitated and shrugged.

'How do you get a passport?' he said.

She was going to Italy. And now that she had that and the weekends at Rosewilder to look forward to, school became bearable. Even when her antennae began to tell her, quite unmistakably, that another barbecue was planned at Codgerley to which she was not invited, the hurt didn't bite too deeply. She had a feeling that things were going to change, that she was going to give everyone a big surprise, though she wasn't as yet very definite as to what it would be.

In particular, she hugged the thought of surprising Raine. Because, when all was said and done, Raine mattered more than anything. More even than Italy, more than any of the things she had told Mrs Considine she wanted. When she came to think of it, there was something in what Mrs Considine had said about these things being 'shallow'. Wonderful though they were in themselves, their greatest value would be in making herself interesting and exciting to Raine . . .

Twice more she went to Rosewilder at weekends. She sailed and rode Pippin again and Anne introduced her to tennis. She had hoped to go in the pool and try to improve her swimming – which wasn't very good – but the weather wasn't warm enough yet.

She was excited to find that her confidence was growing all the time. No longer did she feel clumsy and dimwitted when Anne showed her something. Never having been good at anything in particular she had always tended to assume that it was because she wasn't as capable or as intelligent as other people. Now she began to believe that she could do anything, that it all came down to confidence.

On her third visit to Rosewilder, Alison noticed that Mrs Considine was trying to get her to improve her speech. She didn't need much encouragement. Not wanting to be different from the others in her class, most of whom spoke very well, she had for some time made a conscious effort to imitate them. All Mrs Considine seemed to want her to do was to get into the habit of speaking more confidently, a little more loudly and pronouncing each word more distinctly.

Alison's early gratitude to Mrs Considine was beginning to become worship.

Then on the Saturday that the half-term began she walked out of 2, Holtwood Lane, palpitating with excitement, gave a last exuberant wave to her family who were watching from the doorway, and was picked up at the corner by Michael in the Rolls.

She was taken to Rosewilder where her luggage for the Italian holiday, all of it consisting of Camilla Considine's belongings, was waiting. She handed her new passport to Mrs Considine. Before setting off for London Airport however, she found herself unexpectedly swept off by Mrs Considine to the nearby town of Ardington where Julian, a hairdresser whose fame had reached even Alison's ears, was ready and waiting, under the close direction of Mrs Considine, to reshape her hair.

Back to Rosewilder where, now in such a state of confused and happy shock that she hardly knew what was going on, she put on a skirt and jumper of Camilla's before climbing into the car once more for the two hour journey to London Airport, there to board a plane that thundered into the sky bound for Italy.

She had, from time to time, heard Jenny Allingham complaining about how fearfully boring it was to travel by plane and hang around airports. To Jenny Allingham, maybe, but not to her. The whole process was one of non-stop, second-by-second feverish thrill.

It was in Italy that Alison really changed.

9
Bewitched

They travelled southwards from Rome in a car hired by Mrs Considine. She was a fast driver and clearly knew the route well. Alison sat beside her, enraptured, looking out of the window at the fierce sunshine, drinking in all the unfamiliar sights and sounds. It was, by now, beginning to seem quite natural to her to play the role of Ca Considine.

In the evening, when the sun was losing its heat, they turned down a road that twisted corkscrew-like around and between mountains and Alison saw, beyond the olive groves and vineyards, a dazzling white and pink town perched above a harbour and a brilliant blue sea. Through the town and past the harbour Mrs Considine drove until she came to a white hotel which stood by itself at the head of a beach looking straight towards the sea and the setting sun. When Alison got out of the car there was a tropical feel to the place. It was the feeling of deep warmth that was there despite the time of day and the earliness of the month, the subtle scents from the vegetation and the cicadas which were singing all round them.

The manager must have been summoned immediately they arrived because he appeared almost straight away, a tall, dignified man who seemed to know Mrs Considine well. He took one of her hands in both of his and kissed her on both cheeks and then, somewhat to Alison's embarrassment, he turned to her and did the same. In between kisses he was saying how nice it was to meet again and that she would have the same room as always.

Alison took it that he was saying this to Mrs Considine. She noticed that Mrs Considine was watching her with that smile of hers.

A meal had been prepared just for the two of them and they ate on the terrace, Alison gazing along the line of headlands which stretched blue to the horizon and listening to the faint sound of a mandoline coming from inside the hotel. A balmy breeze was playing on her cheek. It was very hard for her to believe this was all happening. Then she went to bed in a room on the first floor next to Mrs Considine's. It was pink-washed with its own basin and a balcony with a vine growing over it. She had never slept in a room like this before.

She awoke at dawn the following morning from sheer excitement and lay for hours revelling in the luxury and prettiness of it all.

On that first day Mrs Considine encouraged her to explore her surroundings, the beach and the town. There were a few other people on the beach and in the sea, some water skiing, some diving or sailing. Mrs Considine remarked sadly that some day the avalanche of tourists must hit it, but so far the place had changed hardly at all in the ten years that she had known it, perhaps because the approach road was so tortuous and precipitous.

Alison heard no other voices speaking English on the beach. They were all Italian or what she guessed to be German or Swedish or Danish. There were some boys and girls of her own age. She splashed joyously in the shallow water and promised herself that here in these delicious surroundings she really would make an effort to learn to swim properly. Equipped with a hired snorkel tube and mask she spent half the morning gazing at the coral and fishes under the surface. Jenny Allingham, with all her talk about pollution, had never mentioned such wonders as this. Presumably she just took it for granted that everyone knew.

Mrs Considine seemed anxious only that Alison should enjoy herself. She herself ventured into the water only once, for a short swim.

'I'd have liked to help you with your swimming, Ca,' she said, 'but I'd probably only show you bad habits, I'm not very good myself. One length of the pool and I'm exhausted.'

Mrs Considine was calling her 'Ca' all the time, even in the presence of other people. Alison hardly noticed. She was, after all, wearing a bathing suit belonging to Camilla Considine and she was conscious that her new hair style, thrust upon her so suddenly and unexpectedly, made her look more like the real Camilla than ever.

Here, remote from home, it was easier to accept such things than it had been in England.

In the afternoon they explored the town and Alison bought a picture postcard to send home. Mrs Considine had walked on a little way while she chose it and Alison, glancing round to see where she'd got to, saw her as if she were a stranger again.

She had paused by a shop to glance at some pictures which were displayed on racks on the pavement. She was wearing a pale green dress with white dots on it and a broad-brimmed, rather floppy white hat, beneath which her face still looked pale and cool, quite unaffected by the burning sun. Alison thought how elegant and beautiful and even a little mysterious she looked, and she experienced a sudden feeling of deep pride and wonder that she should be associated with her, that they were there together.

At that moment, Mrs Considine glanced back at her and smiled and the sense of pride and wonder became overwhelming. When, at a counter in the post office a few minutes later, she came to try to write on the picture postcard, she found that she had an absolute block against doing so. It was as if she didn't want to be reminded of who she really was. She made it as brief as possible, simply saying *Got here safely, having a lovely time, love Alison* – as if it were a cable, then stuck it hastily in the box and forgot about it.

But later on that afternoon, for the first time, she felt a little afraid of what was happening. It was when they arrived back at the hotel. The manager was standing by a table on the terrace, chatting to a man and woman who were sitting there. Seeing Mrs Considine and Alison approaching he called to them.

'I should like you to meet Mr and Mrs Martin,' he said to them. 'They're from America. They were just saying they felt a little lonely without any of their fellow country-men here, and I said I couldn't produce any Americans but what about some splendid English people?'

'And we said that'd be at least as good,' said Mr Martin gallantly, in a courteous Southern drawl, rising to shake hands.

'Just at the very moment you appeared round the corner,' said Mrs Martin.

'Which just shows you how prompt our service is,' beamed the manager. 'Mr and Mrs Martin have a daughter of Camilla's age, too. It might be nice for the two girls to get together.'

With this he laid a friendly hand on Alison's shoulder.

She had become so accustomed to being addressed as 'Ca' that, for a moment, it didn't quite dawn upon Alison what he had said but when it did, it was a shock.

'I've known Camilla almost all her life,' he was saying, still keeping his hand on her shoulder. 'You've come here every year for – oh, it must be ten years now, mustn't it?'

He thought she was Camilla Considine! And Mrs Considine had let him think so. She was looking at Alison now with a strange expression on her face, a pensive, quirky half-smile. But a sad smile. She clearly had no intention of putting the manager right. Nor did she look as if she were expecting Alison to do so.

'Our daughter's called Louisa,' said Mrs Martin. 'She's down on the beach somewhere. I guess she'll be thrilled to have a friend while she's on holiday.'

'Here she comes now,' grinned Mr Martin. A perky looking, red-haired girl in a swimming suit with a towel slung over her shoulder was coming on to the terrace.

Alison was slowly recovering from the shock. She had had an odd, scared feeling for a moment but that was going now. Returning to take its place was the feeling of pride and wonder at being associated with Mrs Considine. To be taken for her daughter was all right by her. More than all right, in fact. Who cared why Mrs Considine was doing it, or what the real Camilla would think if she knew? Let the future look after itself.

'Louisa, dear,' said Mrs Martin, 'here's a new friend for you. Why don't you two go off and get to know each other?'

'Hi,' said Louisa, looking Alison up and down in a friendly way.

'Hallo,' replied Alison.

'What's your name?' asked Louisa with engaging directness.

Alison glanced at Mrs Considine out of the corner of her eye. Mrs Considine was still looking at her, pensively.

'Camilla Considine,' said Alison, clearly and defiantly. 'Ca to my friends.'

'You don't know how much of a thrill this gives me to be looking for shells with somebody from the English upper classes,' said Louisa. 'I never thought I'd actually meet somebody who was called "Ca".'

It was an hour later. The girls were collecting sea shells and coral, paddling about in the shallow water. Alison was enjoying herself.

'I've only ever heard the name once before,' said Louisa, 'and that was in a book. She was the girlfriend of your English poet, Rupert Brooke. But she spelt hers K – A. Short for Katherine, maybe?'

'I suppose so,' said Alison, who'd never heard of her.

'It's so romantic,' said Louisa. 'What did you say the name of your house was?'

'Rosewilder.'

'Rosewilder,' breathed Louisa. 'Has it got big lawns – and ponies – and a rose garden – and acres of grounds – ?'

'It's got fourteen acres altogether,' said Alison, gravely – Anne had mentioned that fact to her – 'and it's by the shore of a big lake.'

Louisa sat down on a rock and stared at her with deep respect.

'You must think I'm dull,' she said. 'We live in a city house – in Atlanta.'

'That sounds very romantic to me,' said Alison.

Louisa snorted. 'I always heard the English upper classes were great on tact,' she said.

'Well, if you think my home sounds so marvellous,' said Alison recklessly, 'you must come and visit us some day.'

In Italy, Alison had become Camilla Considine. She entered into the role more than willingly. It was as if she had been bewitched and enchanted by Mrs Considine. Not by the use of magic but simply by making her day-dreams come true.

During the course of the week she made other friends besides Louisa. There was a German boy called Kurt and a Finnish girl called Lena. Both spoke English fluently.

The four of them went around as a gang. Alison had never had this many friends before and for her it was a thrilling new experience to find that she seemed to be regarded as the leader. Instead of feeling shy, she found herself chattering freely. Her confidence had grown enormously, so much so that to look back at the gauche Alison Allbright of only a few days ago was like looking back at a different person.

Partly it was the holiday atmosphere that had brought this about. But, more than that, it was the confidence that came from being Camilla Considine.

It was as if, having hovered between the two personalities, she had now crossed the divide.

During the week, Mrs Considine encouraged her all the time to make friends, to do things. It was like being on holiday with the perfect mother of her dreams.

There lurked, somewhere at the back of her mind, disquieting thoughts. Why was Mrs Considine doing this? And what *would* the real Camilla Considine think about it if she knew? Anyway, why had Mrs Considine come here without her real daughter for the first time in ten years? If her half-term fell during a different week, why hadn't she arranged to come then?'

However, Alison didn't allow these thoughts to emerge from her subconscious very often. She was bewitched and enchanted and wanted to stay that way.

On the following Saturday, after saying goodbye to her new friends with emotional, if insincere, promises to meet again sometime, Alison flew back home to England with Mrs Considine. Home – to Rosewilder.

10
Alison Goes to the Barbecue

Alison had gone to Italy as one person. She came back another.

Michael was waiting for them at London Airport and Alison flung herself into the rear corner of the Rolls-Royce and waited while he put the luggage in the boot as if she had been doing it all her life. She was shutting her mind to the thought that within a few hours' time she would be back in Number 2, Holtwood Lane, Alison Allbright once more. She would not face that until it happened. Not one moment before.

'Did you have a nice time?' Michael asked as he drove away.

'Oh, yes, yes, yes,' said Alison exuberantly. She wasn't at all shy of Michael any more.

'You look different,' he said, squinting at her in the driving mirror. She knew that. She had been looking in mirrors, too. Frequently. Her face had become brown with the sun, of course, but that was only to be expected. It was much more than that. Her new hair style contributed to the difference. It had been cunningly shaped to fall crisply and rather mischievously round her face. Sometimes it would blow wispily right over the face but a toss of the head and a touch of her hand would send it back into place again.

But it was more than that, too. The big difference was in her expression. The morose, shrinking look which she had struggled so long and unsuccessfully to get rid of had somehow simply evaporated of its own accord. The fact that she had been living with zest and confidence for a week expressed itself in her face.

It was nice to be in England again. After they had left the motorway and the main roads behind and had turned into the narrow country roads which led to Rosewilder, she saw that during the week they had been away the leaves had grown and the hedgerows had become lush and dense. When she opened the window a little she could smell the may blossom.

They arrived at Rosewilder in the early evening. For Alison it was as if she had come home. Anne was waiting for them as they got out of the car, all smiles, offering tea and asking whether they would like a meal prepared. Mrs Considine said they'd been eating themselves silly on the aeroplane and not to worry about food for a while yet.

Before having tea, Alison couldn't resist slipping up to Camilla's room to look at the photograph once more. Picking it up she glanced from it to her own reflection in the mirror and then back again. They seemed uncannily alike now. It could have been a photograph of herself.

Oddly, she didn't feel jealous of the real Camilla any more, perhaps because her confidence in herself had grown so much. The other Camilla seemed at times so remote, so almost forgotten about, that Alison had come to feel on equal terms with her. Perhaps as a rival she could be beaten, after all. Perhaps she wasn't even a rival, more of a friend.

Alison smiled at the photograph and put it down.

When she came downstairs, she met Anne and Michael coming out of the drawing room, Anne carrying an empty tray. Michael was muttering something to her but broke off as he saw Alison.

'I've just left some tea in there for you,' said Anne, with the same deference that she always showed. But Alison thought she looked rather flushed, almost as if she had been having a quarrel with somebody. Could Mrs Considine have been telling her off, perhaps?

Nothing could have seemed less likely when Alison entered the drawing room. Mrs Considine was standing by the window, sipping tea and looking out at the garden.

'Let's drink this quickly and go out there,' she said to Alison. 'I'm impatient to see how the garden's coming on.

Apparently it's been warm while we've been away and everything's simply blossoming.'

The garden was full of the scent of wallflowers and lilac and azaleas.

'Is it nice to be home?' asked Mrs Considine as they walked together along the path bordered on either side by a lavender hedge.

'Yes,' said Alison, and meant it. She was still bewitched.

'Oh, look,' said Mrs Considine, pausing to take a yellow rose in her hand, 'the first of the shrub roses are out.'

Alison breathed in the warm, fragrant air and gazed at the lake. The water was darkening as the sun sank lower. In the distance she could see the still darker belt of trees on the opposite shore. It was Saturday. She wondered if the boaty crowd had been along there today –

A pinprick of fire, growing larger, was suddenly to be seen among the trees.

'The barbecue!' exclaimed Alison. 'It's tonight they're having the barbecue. They've just lit the fire.'

In spite of everything, she could still feel a stab of hurt at being excluded.

Mrs Considine seemed to wake from a reverie. She looked across the lake. 'You mean the people you told me about?' she asked. 'The "boaty crowd" as you call them?'

Alison nodded. 'Raine will be there.'

Mrs Considine gazed across the lake.

'Then let us go, too,' she said.

'Us?' said Alison, amazed. 'But we can't. I mean we're not invited. And anyway I – ' Then she remembered what Mrs Considine had said to her about keeping things secret 'just a little while longer – maybe until you come back from Italy . . .'

'Do you mean I can go and see Raine and tell her?' she said excitedly. 'About coming here and going to Italy and – '

'I mean, Ca,' said Mrs Considine patiently and slowly, as if explaining something very obvious to someone very stupid, 'that I would like to take you to the barbecue and introduce you to them as my daughter. I'm quite sure they would make you welcome.'

Alison looked at Mrs Considine.

She was enchanted and bewitched and intoxicated by what had happened to her here at Rosewilder and in Italy. She had become accustomed to thinking of herself as Camilla Considine rather than Alison Allbright. But to present herself to Raine and the others in that role! That was something different again.

'I can't do that,' she whispered.

Mrs Considine turned away from her. She took the stem of the yellow rose between thumb and forefinger and carefully broke it off. Then she held it beneath her nose and looked at Alison over the top of it while breathing in the perfume.

'You must, Ca.'

It was an order. It brooked no refusal.

Alison knew that she had arrived, perhaps not so much at a crossroads but at a one-way barrier through which, once passed, she would not be able to return.

She longed to pass the barrier. She wanted to be Camilla Considine. She had always wanted that. It was the sum of all her day-dreams. But she couldn't. She didn't dare . . .

'There is a white dress in the wardrobe,' said Mrs Considine. 'I think you should wear that and I will pin the one yellow rose on the shoulder.'

. . . but if she didn't dare, she would be in the car back to Holtwood Lane. Her day-dreams would be nothing but day-dreams again.

'They'll all be in jeans and sweaters,' she found herself saying weakly.

'Jeans and sweaters may be all right for them but not for Camilla Considine. You will glow and shimmer in the firelight like a pearl. You will be the centre of attention.'

She couldn't stand against Mrs Considine's will.

Mrs Considine drove the car herself while Alison sat beside her in the white dress, a white shawl about her shoulders. At the Sturridge-Ardington road they turned right towards Codgerley again and as they neared the lake the glare of the bonfire could be seen through the trees. The car nosed down the track leading to the pier. Mrs Considine parked it behind another one and they got out.

Alison saw the figures moving against the firelight and heard shouts and laughter. She was frightened almost to the point of terror.

As they came into the clearing the first person she saw was Susannah Strickland. She was eating a sausage while chatting and laughing animatedly with a boy. She glanced round as Alison entered the clearing and her eyes widened as she saw her. She said something to the boy, who looked round, too. At the other end of the clearing, near the lake, adults were cooking sausages and hamburgers on a grid over the fire which had been visible from Rosewilder. In the deep shade of the trees they were little more than silhouettes against the glow of the fire. Alison saw that Raine was among them, back towards her, kneeling, apparently trying to make toast against some of the hot ashes.

The shadows, the drifting wood-smoke, the lanterns hanging amongst the trees illuminating the lush green foliage – all combined to produce an exotic, almost primeval atmosphere.

Alison saw that Mr and Mrs Woodward were moving towards them inquiringly.

'Good evening,' said Mrs Considine at her most charming. 'My daughter and I live on the other side of the lake.' She nodded in the direction of Rosewilder. 'We saw your fire and couldn't resist coming for a closer look.'

'Come and have a sausage,' beamed Mrs Woodward. 'You are – ?'

'Mrs Considine and this is my daughter, Camilla.'

How easy for Mrs Considine to gatecrash! It didn't even seem like gatecrashing.

Alison had been fully expecting the Woodwards to recognize her. But there was no sign of that. Admittedly they didn't know her very well and she now looked different, but even so . . .

Her terror subsided a little. It was dawning upon her that if you were bold enough – the bolder the better – you could get away with anything. People accepted you for what you told them you were. Mrs Considine knew that.

'We'll just stay for a few minutes,' Mrs Considine was saying. 'My daughter thought it looked such fun. She's just come back from school in Switzerland and she doesn't know anybody around here.' She glanced about her.

'Why don't you wander around and meet people, Camilla?'

She started chatting to the Woodwards again, turning her back on Alison who, bereft of her support, suddenly felt exposed and panic-stricken once more.

The figures about her were taking on the identities of people she knew. That was Jenny Allingham over there, looking at her. And Katie Lee and Robert Simes. They were *all* looking at her. Mrs Considine had said she would be the centre of attention and she had been right. In her shining white dress and shawl she felt like a beacon. Surely they'd start laughing in a moment and start calling her name, Alison Allbright.

But they weren't laughing. As far as she could tell, the glances were of curiosity. *Be bold and people till take you for what you tell them you are. I am Camilla Considine.*

Susannah Strickland was coming towards her.

'I think we've met before,' said Susannah. 'Aren't you –' she paused momentarily and Alison cringed – 'Camilla Considine?'

'I'm afraid I don't remember you,' Alison replied and she walked away before Susannah could see that she was trembling. She had said that simply so as to be able to escape as quickly as possible, but then it dawned upon her that it had been the perfect response. It was a dream come true. She had snubbed Susannah Strickland. She almost wanted to laugh from excitement and relief. Her confidence was back.

She found that she was walking towards the fire. Raine was still kneeling, back towards her, still trying to get the same piece of bread to brown.

There was a table nearby with some cut bread on it and Alison took a piece and impaled it on a fork. Then she went and stood behind Raine.

'That seems like a good idea. I think I'll make some toast, too,' she said.

'Not such a good idea as all that,' said Raine, without looking up to see who it was. 'Even if it ever does get brown, which doesn't seem very likely at the moment, it's going to be covered in ash.'

'Still, it's worth a try,' said Alison and placing her shawl on the ground she knelt down on it, beside her, holding the bread out towards the edge of the fire. Raine glanced round.

And stared. At Alison's face glowing in the firelight and at the gleaming white dress.

'My name's Camilla Considine,' said Alison. Her voice seemed to be coming from outside herself. 'My mother's over there.' She pointed her piece of bread in the direction of Mrs Considine, who was now moving about, nodding and smiling and exchanging words with people.

'Oh, *you're* Camilla Considine,' exclaimed Raine, still staring. 'That explains it.'

'Explains what?' said Alison, keeping her gaze on the bread which she had now returned to its position in front of the fire.

'You look just like – like somebody I know. You even sound a bit like her. It's quite uncanny. A girl called Alison Allbright. You wouldn't know her, I suppose.'

'I – er – I don't think so,' replied Alison cautiously. She hadn't been prepared for that question. 'I think my mother may have met her.'

Raine looked round at Mrs Considine and smiled. 'I doubt it,' she said. 'I didn't really seriously think you'd know her. I've heard of you, though. Susannah Strickland told me about you. Said you were the image of Alison.'

'Susannah *who*?' said Alison, with a curl of the lip. She didn't know where all this was taking her, but she wasn't nervous any longer. She was starting to have a feeling of great elation and at the same time of great peace, as if this situation were satisfying something deep inside her.

'Strickland. A girl I know.' Raine seemed to have examined Alison's face to her satisfaction. She turned her attention back to her toast. 'Where do you go to school?'

'Switzerland,' said Alison. Then, remembering what Mrs

90

Considine had said to the Woodwards, she added, 'I have been, that is. I've just come back from there.'

'Oh, blow!' said Raine. 'I've just got some more ash on it. I keep on asking myself whether a piece of toast is worth all this trouble. I think I'll eat mine now and get rid of it. How's yours?'

'As much worth eating as it's ever going to be.'

It was a warm and cosy feeling to be with Raine. When Mrs Considine came and stood over them a few minutes later they were chatting and laughing together and munching ashy toast with sausages.

'I think we ought to get back now, Ca,' she said to them. 'We don't want to overstay our welcome.'

'Oh, but – ' began both girls simultaneously.

'I've been inviting everyone to a party at Rosewilder next Saturday,' said Mrs Considine, 'to celebrate your home-coming, Ca.' She ignored the look of astonishment on Alison's face. 'Would your friend – ?' She paused.

'Raine,' said Raine.

'Would Raine like to come too?'

Everything was totally out of hand now.

'Thank you,' Raine was saying eagerly, 'I'd love that. How do you get to – what was it – Rosewilder?'

Alison listened mutely as Mrs Considine described the route. Then Mrs Considine took her arm.

'Till next week then,' Mrs Considine smiled to Raine, 'at six o'clock.'

Alison was led away.

'There is one person I haven't asked,' said Mrs Considine, pausing and frowning. 'That blonde girl over there – she's looking at us now while pretending not to. I thought I would check with you because her name is – oh, I've forgotten it again – but I seem to remember your telling me she wasn't very nice, something like that.'

It was Susannah Strickland.

'No, don't ask *her*,' said Alison, suddenly laughing. 'Come on, let's go.' She added, as an afterthought, 'Let's go home, Mummy' – and laughed again.

With a cheerful wave of the hand, Mrs Considine led her away from the firelight, back towards the car.

As they drove back to Rosewilder, some sort of reality returned. Or tried to.

Alison sat with her shawl wrapped round her and looked at the calm profile of Mrs Considine.

'What would Camilla think of this?' she asked.

'You *are* Camilla,' replied Mrs Considine.

'No, I mean the real one, your daughter – '

'You *are* the real one.'

'No, the other one, the proper one whose picture's by the bed – '

'Ca, you must stop this. You are the only Camilla. There is no other. It is your picture that is by the bed.'

'But – but – '

'Now please be quiet, Ca. You must go back to these people for a few days, but then you will come home again.'

11
Homecoming

It was quite late when Alison left Rosewilder. Mrs Considine seemed reluctant to let her go and she herself was in no hurry.

When at last she did step into the Rolls again, to be driven to Holtwood Lane by Micheal, she was in her own clothes once more and her hair was back in its bunches.

She was also clutching some packages, gifts for her family from Italy. They had been handed to her, already wrapped, by Mrs Considine who had produced them from her luggage. They were, apparently, a framed picture for her parents, a pendant for her mother and some Continental chocolates for Keith.

She was surprised and relieved that Mrs Considine had shown such foresight. She had shut her family out of her mind so completely that she had forgotten to buy them any presents herself.

It felt strange, after waving goodbye to Mrs Considine, to settle back in the car and try to adjust herself to being Alison Allbright again. Her clothes, which had once seemed reasonable but now felt indescribably shabby and ill-fitting, and her bunches, which she could see reflected in the car window when she turned her head, should have been enough of a shock to bring her down to earth. But they didn't quite. It still felt more as if she were simply dressing up as Alison Allbright.

Running through her mind all the time was what Mrs Considine had said.

'You are the *only* Camilla . . . it is *your* picture by the bed . . . you must go back to these people for a few days but then you will come home . . .'

What *had* she meant?

Alison wondered whether to ask Michael about the real Camilla. She couldn't quite bring herself to do so.

Ever since her first unsuccessful attempt to question Anne, neither of the Housmans had once volunteered any information about Camilla Considine. Either they had been deliberately secretive or else . . . or else, as Mrs Considine had said, there was no other Camilla . . .

But there had to be! Susannah Strickland had seen her. Why did she keep forgetting that?

Anyway, she couldn't think of a question to put to Michael . . .

The car stopped by the corner of Holtwood Lane. He held the door open for her while she got out.

'Thank you, goodnight,' she said and putting her packages inside her holdall started to walk away. He didn't move, however, and as she was about to turn the corner he called: 'Just a minute.'

She stopped and looked around.

'It doesn't matter,' he said. He got into the car, reversed into the lane, then drove away back towards Rosewilder.

Lightning flashed in the distance and a few drops of rain fell as Alison walked along the lane, pondering what it was that he might have been going to say.

There was a light in the living room window. As she lifted the latch of the gate and walked up the short, straight concrete path, the house, the lane, everything, seemed queer and tiny and desolate. The gate banged to behind her and she saw the curtain lift at the side. Her mother was looking out.

She opened the front door and there in front of her was the tiny hall and the bleak, precipitous staircase rising from it. It all looked utterly depressing. The door to the living room opened.

'Alison!' said her mother. 'We've been getting so worried about you.'

She backed away to let Alison in. The living room looked the size of a large box. Seated in one of the armchairs was Alison's father, laying his newspaper down on his knees to look at her. There was an atmosphere of worry and disapproval.

She noticed that her postcard from Italy was propped up in the centre of the mantelpiece.

'Worried?' she said, standing in the doorway of the living room. 'Why?'

'Oh, it doesn't matter now,' said her mother, 'just as long as you're back safely.'

'Why shouldn't I be?' asked Alison, irritably. It was bad enough having to come back here at all without being made to feel guilty about it into the bargain.

'Hallo, Alison,' said her father. He looked as if he were trying to be friendly. 'Did you have a good time?'

'Yes, Dad.'

'Well, that's all that matters, isn't it?' said her mother, more comfortably. 'Would you like a cup of tea and something to eat?'

'No thanks,' said Alison. She was fighting a feeling of wanting to explode. 'Look, I've brought you some presents from Italy.' She placed her packages on the table. 'The big one's for both of you, the little one's a special present for Mum and this is something for Keith. Where is Keith?'

'In bed,' said her father. 'It's quite late you know.'

'That's nice,' said Mrs Allbright, looking at the packages brightly. 'Shall I open the one that's for both of us?'

'That's what they're there for,' said Alison, trying to sound jolly.

Mrs Allbright opened the biggest package first. The picture was a small landscape in a gilt frame. She scrutinized it closely before laying it carefully on the table.

There was a silence. Then:

'*You* didn't choose that, did you, Alison?' said her father heavily.

As a gift for the Allbrights it was ludicrous. The landscape was exquisite but it would have looked as out of place in their living room as china ducks on the wall of the National Gallery.

Mrs Considine had been unable to lower her taste to that of the Allbrights.

'It must have cost a lot of money,' said Alison's mother. She opened the smallest package.

The pendant, like a tear drop on a gold chain, consisted of a blue stone surrounded by smaller stones which looked like diamonds.

Mrs Allbright fingered it, not knowing what to say.

'Where's she going to wear that?' asked Alison's father, who did.

The stones which looked like diamonds really were diamonds and the blue one was a sapphire. The pendant would have cost at least £2,500 in the shops, probably more. But Mr and Mrs Allbright didn't know that. Nor did Alison. They took it for granted that it was a nice imitation.

Mr Allbright had been watching Alison. He stood up, laying his paper aside. 'You've never seen those things before, have you?' he said brusquely. 'It's not just that you didn't choose them yourself. You've never even *seen* them.'

'Now, John – ' began Mrs Allbright, defensively, ' – now don't you shout.'

'I'm not shouting. First of all she can't be bothered to write a proper letter and let us know what she's doing. Then she hands us some things that woman's bought for us. Like paying off the servants!' His voice was rising steadily.

He picked up the picture and the pendant and put them in the wall cupboard to the left of the fireplace. Things put in there were usually forgotten forever.

'They're wasted on you all right,' muttered Alison, savagely.

'Don't be cheeky, Alison,' said her mother sharply.

Her father stood by the fireplace, drumming his finger-tips on the mantelpiece.

'Have you come straight here from the airport?' he demanded suddenly.

She almost decided to say 'yes' but she was too confused and, anyway, he wouldn't have believed her.

'No,' she said.

'You've been at Rosewilder, haven't you? With your rich friend.'

'So what?'

'Look at it from our point of view, Alison,' said her mother. 'We let you go off abroad with somebody who's really a total stranger to us. You don't let us know how you're getting on. When you get back you don't turn up till late . . .'

'And to cap it all,' said her father, 'you bring us some presents that you've never even seen before we unwrapped them.' He was keeping his temper only with the greatest effort.

So was Alison. So she'd hurt them! What did they expect? What had they ever done for her? If she'd been brought up badly, who'd brought her up?

In the brief silence, Alison heard a movement on the stairs.

'Keith,' shouted her father. 'Is that you? Come here.'

Some reluctant footfalls on the stairs and the door was pushed open. Keith stood there in his pyjamas, looking, Alison thought, ridiculous. His pyjamas were far too small for him and the trousers came to an end at mid-calf.

'What are you doing out of bed?' shouted Mr Allbright, clearly near snapping point.

'I heard the noise,' mumbled Keith. 'I just wanted to see what was going on.'

'Alison's got a present for you from Italy. I expect it's bath salts.'

Alison snapped.

'Have it now,' she shouted. 'I'll show you what it is.'

She ripped off the wrapping and, trembling, yanked the lid off the box inside to reveal rows of dark Continental chocolates. They would probably be much appreciated by connoisseurs but Keith wasn't a connoisseur. He only liked milk chocolates.

'There you are,' she screamed. 'There's your present from Italy.' She hurled the lot at him.

The next moment her father had her by the wrist and,

97

face contorted, she was struggling furiously to get away from him.

'That's it,' he said. 'That's the last time you go and see that woman. Never, never again.'

She was about to yell at him that he was wrong, that nothing and nobody would prevent her from seeing Mrs Considine again, when suddenly she changed her mind. She became limp.

What made her change her mind was partly the realization that she couldn't hope to win by directly challenging her father. Her best bet was to be cunning and lull him into a false sense of security.

It was more than that, though. What made her able to contemplate being cunning with such equanimity was that she had a sudden overwhelming feeling of detachment. From her father. From her mother. From Keith. From this house. From herself.

She didn't want to be Alison Allbright any more. She rejected her.

What was it that Mrs Considine had said?

You are Camilla . . . there is no other . . . you must go back to these people for a few days then you will come home . . .

She was Camilla Considine. She was staying, inexplicably, in this house with these people who were treating her as if she were a member of their family called Alison. She would tolerate this till next Saturday, when she would go home to Rosewilder. Beyond that she couldn't see, but that didn't matter.

Until then she must be cunning.

'I shan't be going back to Rosewilder anyway,' she said sullenly.

Her father let go of her wrist. But he was still suspicious.

'Why not?' he asked.

'Because Camilla Considine has come back from Switzerland,' said Alison, 'and she doesn't want me at Rosewilder.'

Out of the corner of her eye she could see relief on her mother's face.

'You mean the two of you don't get on, after all?' asked Mrs Allbright.

'That's right,' said Alison. 'Camilla Considine and Alison Allbright don't mix. I'm going to bed.'

She started towards the door, stepping over the scattered chocolates. Keith was still standing by the door staring.

'Just a minute, Alison,' said her father. She paused.

'I'm sorry for your sake that you won't be going back,' he said stiffly, not looking at her, 'because I know you've been having a good time there. But I think it's just as well. I'm sorry I got a bit rough.'

She nodded and walked past Keith and up the stairs. These people didn't matter.

Alison was still bewitched.

12
The Truth about Camilla

It was the same at school.

She didn't want to be Alison Allbright sitting unnoticed at one side of the classroom or mooching around by herself in the grounds during break periods. To do these things was only tolerable if she could believe that she was really Ca Considine having to spend a week unaccountably pretending to be this wretched Alison Allbright, but that at the end of it she would return to being her proper self again.

What would happen after that party at Rosewilder on Saturday, she didn't think about. It was as if a high wall lay beyond that, over which she could not and did not want to see.

It wasn't as if the confidence she had found as Ca Considine stayed with her when she became Alison Allbright again. That melted away. Even her facial expression reverted to normal. Once back in her usual routine, confronted by the familiar everyday situations that she had always been used to, the habits and fears of Alison Allbright reasserted themselves.

Despite that, it was a fascinating week. As she took her place in assembly first thing on Monday morning she noticed that she was being looked at and whispered about by several people. Obviously they were comparing her with the 'Camilla Considine' they had seen at the barbecue.

Glancing round, she was momentarily disconcerted to see Raine gazing at her from the row behind and wondered if she had realized the truth. But then Raine looked away without giving any sign of recognition. She had merely been staring into space.

There was a PE lesson that morning and while Alison was queuing up to vault over the box – which she hated deeply and almost always muffed – she found herself behind Raine and Susannah Strickland whom she had noticed chatting together in short bursts.

' – just an oversight,' she heard Raine say. 'Stop worrying. I'm sure she meant to ask everybody.'

It dawned upon her what they were talking about, and she almost burst out laughing. Susannah had found out that everybody at the barbecue except her had been invited to Camilla Considine's party. And it hurt. She wanted to go.

That made Alison's morning. She vaulted the box quite well.

It also proved to her that Raine had been completely taken in by 'Camilla Considine'. She wondered if Susannah Strickland would try to turn up at Rosewilder. That would be fun.

At lunch time Stephen Kirkpatrick, hunched over his place, elbows on table, fixed her with his eyes.

'Saw somebody who looks like you on Saturday – ' he began, then stopped in some confusion. Jenny Allingham had apparently kicked him under the table. She must have remembered to have some finer feelings about Alison's not having been invited to the barbecue.

Alison carried on eating.

'What did you do over half-term, Breezy?' he asked her, recovering. 'Go anywhere exciting?'

She didn't look up.

'Great conversationalist, our Breezy,' he said. 'I look forward to lunch times and our stimulating discussions. Stick around, the rest of you, and just drink it all in.'

'I flew to Italy for a few days,' said Alison.

He laid his knife and fork down on the table and stared at her open-mouthed.

'Did you hear that?' he said. '*Did you hear that*? She's brilliant enough when she doesn't speak. Just to watch her expression is enough! But when she talks as well – what wit – what – '

'Keep your voice down, that boy over there,' commanded Mr Weatherall, the duty master, passing by.

Alison hadn't even noticed Stephen at the barbecue, but apparently he'd been there. So it was more than likely that Mrs Considine had asked him to Rosewilder. What a bizarre thought!

She could take Stephen Kirkpatrick and anything else, now that she had Saturday to look forward to.

But what *would* happen after Saturday?

What *had* Mrs Considine really meant about her being the only Camilla?

On Thursday afternoon, as Alison was cycling home from school on her new bike, she saw a uniformed figure standing at the corner of Eastgate Street and the High Street. It was Michael Housman. He waved her down.

The sight frightened her. 'Is something wrong?' she asked him, as she stopped.

He looked along Eastgate Street. There were no other High School uniforms in sight. The buses had gone.

'Come into the Stewpot for a few minutes,' he said.

The Stewpot was a café a short distance away along the High Street. Having parked her bike outside, Alison took a seat on one of the brown, leather-covered benches. Michael got a coffee and an orange drink from the counter, then sat down opposite her.

'I've come here without Mrs Considine's permission,' he said, 'and she wouldn't be very pleased if she knew. I'd rather you didn't tell her.'

'Oh,' said Alison. She didn't know what else to say.

'However, Anne and I decided it was my duty to come. I nearly said something to you last Saturday, but I thought I ought to talk it over with her first.' He hesitated. 'You must understand it's very difficult for me to say this. Mrs Considine's our employer and she's always been very good to us. We have a great respect for her and we wouldn't want to do anything against her wishes, but . . .'

Alison had a cold fear inside her. She had been afraid,

from the moment of first seeing him, that his coming to meet her boded ill.

'. . . well, it's all got out of hand. We did wonder about seeing your parents, but it's so much better if this can be kept between ourselves.'

'What do you mean?' asked Alison tautly. 'What's got out of hand?' As if she didn't know!

'We think,' he said, 'that you should telephone Mrs Considine straight away and tell her that you won't be coming back to Rosewilder again, that you won't ever see her again. Will you promise me you'll do that?'

So there it was. She had been right to be afraid.

He leaned back, relaxing a little. He seemed to feel that he had said enough and to be waiting for her to agree. But she wasn't going to let him get away with that.

She rested her chin on her fists and looked at the tablecloth. 'Why should I?' she said.

'Look,' he said, tolerantly, 'you've taken Mrs Considine's games in very good part and I'm sure you've found it fun. I can understand that. I was brought up in the East End myself, in Bow, and if some wealthy person had decided to treat me as their son and heap lots of goodies on me, I don't suppose I'd have asked too many questions. Not at first, anyway.

'As for Anne and me, we've been joining in the games as well, for Mrs Considine's sake. We thought it best for her. But now it's like I said. It's gone too far. You must know that as well as I do.'

Alison went on staring at the tablecloth.

'Have you said anything about this to Mrs Considine?' she asked.

'We um – we tried,' he said.

So they hadn't got anywhere with her. Alison wondered if that was why Anne had looked so strained on the evening they had returned from Italy. Perhaps she and Mrs Considine had been quarrelling then.

'I still don't see what you mean about things having gone too far,' she said stubbornly, being deliberately obtuse.

'Oh, for goodness' sake!' he said, beginning to lose patience. 'Surely you can see you're getting into very deep waters. Surely – '

Then he shrugged. 'Oh, I suppose you've got a right to know the truth,' he said, doubtfully.

'I want to know about Camilla Considine,' said Alison, quick to probe at the first sign of weakness.

He was hesitating. 'You won't noise it around? You realize this is in confidence?'

'I won't noise it around.'

'Camilla Considine is dead.'

Deep down, it didn't come as any great surprise to Alison. Right from the beginning there had been a feeling of *absence* about Camilla Considine. And, of course, Mrs Considine herself had as good as told her. 'You are the only Camilla,' she had said. 'There is no other.'

'How did she die?'

'You promise you won't go telling anybody?'

'I promise.'

Camilla had died in February. It had been a tragedy.

'She started at school in Switzerland last September,' said Michael, 'but Mrs Considine missed her so much that when she came home for the Christmas holidays she wouldn't let her go back. She said she was going to keep her at Rosewilder and have her educated by tutors again . . . but Camilla wanted to get back to Switzerland and in February she ran away. She got an air ticket by forging her mother's signature on a cheque and just turned up at the school.'

'Ran away! She wanted to get back to school that badly!'

'Yes. She was desperate.'

'What did the school do?'

'They telephoned Mrs Considine and she flew straight to Switzerland to bring her back. She was in a terrible fury. It was after she'd collected her from the school that Camilla died. There was an accident . . .'

He paused and stirred his coffee, which so far he hadn't touched, as if wondering whether he ought to go on.

'An accident?' prompted Alison.

'They were travelling from the school back to the airport

104

in a car that Mrs Considine had hired. It was a winding mountain road with a sheer drop to one side, and it started to snow heavily. Visibility got very bad and at one point she had to stop when a big lorry came round a bend towards her. Camilla opened the door and jumped out.'

'In the middle of nowhere?'

'I suppose she was hoping to get back to the school somehow. Anyway, Mrs Considine jammed on the handbrake and jumped out of the car and ran after her. But she lost sight of her in the snow and Camilla must have slipped or got confused. Anyway, she went over the edge.'

Alison tried to picture the scene; tried to visualize Mrs Considine, so charming and elegant, and Camilla, the confident, attractive girl of the photograph, taking part in that horrible drama on the mountainside. She found it very difficult to do so. It was all too far removed from her world of Holtwood Lane and Sturridge High School.

'But I don't understand,' she said. 'Why was Camilla so desperate to get back to school? She had a marvellous home and mother.'

'Yes, she did,' said Michael. 'But Mrs Considine was very possessive – too possessive. She admitted it afterwards. She'd always worshipped Camilla. She'd hardly let her out of sight, even had her educated at home, till Camilla begged her to let her go to school abroad. Camilla badly wanted to be independent.

'Then after she'd had a taste of freedom, she couldn't take it when Mrs Considine tried to clamp down on her again . . .

'That's what made it so specially terrible for Mrs Considine. She blamed herself. She knew she'd been wrong and she kept on talking about how different things would be if only she could have a second chance . . . except there couldn't be one.

'Then she saw you from a train window when she was coming back from another visit to Switzerland and . . .'

'And what?' said Alison, as he hesitated.

'Well, it was like seeing Camilla born again. To give her that second chance. *You* are her second chance . . .

'She didn't work it all out coldly or anything like that.

Things just happened. Mrs Considine is very wealthy and she thinks she can buy anything, even a new Camilla. You.'

He stirred his coffee slowly.

'And Anne and I helped her. Partly because she's our employer and we've got a respect for her, but it was a lot more than that. We were really worried about her. If you could have seen her after Camilla's death . . . we just didn't know what was going to happen. And then you came along and we were just thankful that it comforted her.'

He looked up at Alison.

'But it has to end now. So you just telephone her and say it's goodbye, won't you? It'll be hard on her but it's got to be done. We should never have started it.'

Alison picked up her drink and started to sip it. His eyes were still fixed on her.

'You will tell her, won't you?' he persisted. 'The last thing I want to do is go and see your parents or anybody else, but if I have to – '

'Oh, yes, I'll tell her,' said Alison. 'I was just thinking about what you've told me, that's all: how horrible and strange it all is.'

He looked at her sympathetically. 'Ordinary people like you and me are a bit out of our depth when it comes to dealing with people like Mrs Considine. I've worked for her for about three years now, and I'm very fond of her, but I've still no idea how she ticks.'

Alison felt mildly resentful. She had got used to being treated with deference by the Housmans and she didn't enjoy being suddenly back on a level with them as 'ordinary people' and reminded that the deference had merely been a game.

'I think,' he said, 'that it would be a good idea if you were to make that phone call now and get it over with. I know it's going to be difficult. I'll give you the number. There are some phone boxes outside the post office.'

So he didn't absolutely trust her. He was going to supervise her while she did it and make quite certain that the whole thing came to an end now.

'All right?' he said.

'Yes,' replied Alison.

'Come on then.'

He drank down his coffee and Alison finished her drink.

They walked together to the post office, Alison wheeling her bike. Outside one of the phone boxes he sorted out some change for her and gave her the number. Then he patted her on the shoulder consolingly.

'I expect you're sorry it's got to come to an end, but you've had a nice time, haven't you, especially that holiday in Italy? It couldn't go on for ever.'

He held the door open for her.

'Now remember, you're not asking her anything – she'll try and win you round if you're not firm – you're telling her. And don't mention me.'

He let the door swing to and Alison put a coin in and tapped out the number. Listening to the ringing tone, she looked at Michael out of the corner of her eye. He was walking up and down, watching her.

Came Mrs Considine's voice: 'Hallo. Bradwood Heath 273.'

'Hallo,' she said, 'it's . . . it's . . .' – should she say 'Alison' or 'Ca'?

'Ca!' said Mrs Considine. 'Ca, what a surprise!'

'Michael's outside the phone box,' said Alison. 'He met me coming out of school. He's been telling me everything about – about – well, everything. He told me to telephone you and say that I'm not coming back to Rosewilder ever again. He said I wasn't to tell you he'd seen me.'

'I see,' said Mrs Considine.

'I didn't know what to do. He's watching me now. He thinks I'm doing what he told me.'

'You are doing exactly the right thing, Ca. I hope you're looking forward to your party on Saturday.'

'I'm living for it. But what about Michael – and Anne?'

'Leave that problem entirely to me. I won't let them know that it's you who told me. Oh, and Ca – '

'Yes?'

'There's no need for the Rolls to pick you up on Saturday, is there? You can come on your bike.'

'Yes, of course I can.'

Alison was about to say goodbye when she suddenly remembered something. 'Oh, I wonder if you could invite a girl called Jill Mackenzie to the party. She goes to Sturridge High. I don't know her address but she'll be in the phone book I expect.'

'Certainly, Ca. Till Saturday, then.'

'All right?' asked Michael, as she came out of the phone box.

'Yes,' said Alison.

Michael suddenly grinned ruefully. 'I could see you looking tense,' he said. 'I wasn't envying you. Thank goodness that's over.' Then he became solemn again.

'Not that it *is* all over. We'll have to see how she takes it when it really hits her. I've a feeling Anne and I might be in for a difficult time, but that's not your problem.'

He held out his hand.

'Goodbye. Been nice knowing you. I'll head back up to the car park now.'

Her hand was very limp as he shook it. She watched him as he turned and walked back the way they had come, after giving her a farewell wave. Then she mounted her bike and pedalled slowly homewards.

She was ashamed of having tricked him. But far overriding that was a growing elation. As she cycled along the Ardington Road she tried to suppress the feeling because it was terrible that she was reacting to tragedy in this way. But the elation kept on coming. It was because she knew now that she *was* the only Camilla. She had been unable to see what would happen after the party on Saturday. Now, perhaps, there was a glimmer . . . .

With some pride she reviewed the way she had handled the situation. She had learned to be cunning. The old Alison Allbright wouldn't have kept her wits about her like that.

She wondered what Mrs Considine would do. That was very difficult to imagine, but the problem could be safely left to her.

Alison had absolute faith in Mrs Considine.

13
A Lie Discovered

'I'm off to Codgerley to meet Raine Lawlor,' Alison announced to her parents after lunch on Saturday. 'We're going to swim and maybe do some sailing and after that I've been invited back to her house for tea. I might stay on there afterwards, so I could be late. Don't make me anything.'

'Oh, that's nice,' said her mother. 'You're friends with Raine Lawlor again, are you? I thought that must be all over.'

Mrs Allbright was vague about Alison's relationships since she only ever heard what Alison chose to tell her about them.

'She invited me yesterday,' said Alison. She was glad that Keith had gone into town straight after lunch to visit the library. It would have been less easy to lie with his sardonic gaze fixed upon her, because he must have been aware that she and Raine had remained totally distanced all week. Even so, if it came up later, he wasn't to know that there mightn't have been a sudden end-of-the-week reconciliation.

'Swimming?' said Mr Allbright, who was preparing to watch the sport on television. 'I hope you're not going out of your depth. You're not much of a swimmer, are you?'

'Oh, I improved a lot in Italy,' said Alison lying again. She'd improved a little, but not all that much.

She would have simply told them she was going sailing, but the day had become fiercely hot and sultry without a breath of a breeze. It was unlikely there would be any sailing today and Mr Allbright might realize that.

'It's a relief she's got her friend back again,' said Mrs Allbright after Alison had left the house. 'When I was her age I was always out with friends. I was never indoors.'

'It'll take her mind off that woman, that's the main thing,' said Mr Allbright, easing himself into his chair. 'She seems to have accepted it all right, though.'

It didn't occur to them that Alison, who had never seriously deceived them except for the one occasion when she had gone to Bransome Park with Mrs Considine and had been duly found out and reprimanded, was deceiving them now; that she had become cunning.

With her swimsuit and towel in her saddlebag, for appearances' sake, Alison cycled off along the road to Codgerley. When, some time later, she turned off towards Rosewilder, she increased her speed. She couldn't wait to get there.

She had only one cause for nervousness – meeting the Housmans again. But she had complete faith in Mrs Considine's ability to handle that situation.

There was no one about as she cycled in through the gates, though there was a van parked in front of the house. She hid her bike in the storeroom at the back of the garage. She didn't want anybody from school seeing *that*. The only car in the garage was the Rolls. The red mini which belonged to the Housmans had gone. She hoped that meant they were out.

She entered the house through the side door and slipped quietly up the stairs. She had decided that she didn't want Mrs Considine to see her as Alison Allbright. She wanted to appear to her immediately as Camilla. She was glad therefore to reach Camilla's room unobserved and close the door behind her.

Sunshine was streaming into the room and it looked lovely. She wanted to leap about for sheer joy at being back at Rosewilder again. She went over to the picture of Camilla and studied it, trying to tell herself that this was the face of a girl who had come to a tragic, terrible

110

end, falling down a mountainside in the snow, but somehow that didn't mean anything. It was too much like looking at herself. She and Camilla were more than friends now. They were one.

She heard Mrs Considine's voice outside and she went over to the window and peeped out. The window overlooked the main lawns of the house. Beyond lay gardens and trees and beyond that, Codgerley. Mrs Considine was on the lawn. She had been calling to a man who, perched on a ladder, was putting up fairy lights among the trees. There were trestle tables and chairs on the lawn and another man was bringing more, presumably from the van. There was no sign of the Housmans.

Alison turned away from the window loosening her bunches. She wanted to be rid of Alison Allbright as quickly as possible.

A few minutes later she walked out on to the lawn. She was dressed very simply in some of Camilla's casual clothes: jeans, striped jersey and sandals. But she had become Camilla. Mrs Considine, who was still overseeing preparations for the party, turned and saw her and for a moment became rigid.

'Ca!' she said and she came over and put her arm round her shoulder. Alison knew that she had been right to appear immediately as Camilla.

'It's a beautiful day for the party,' said Mrs Considine, releasing her. 'Just let's hope the thunder holds off. I thought I'd risk having it outside though, and I couldn't resist having some fairy lights.'

She was chattering like a schoolgirl.

'I've asked a catering firm to handle the food and drinks. I expect they'll be here before long. Oh, and I've hired a magician – I hope you don't feel too grown up to have a magician at parties, but I couldn't resist that either. And I've taken the liberty of inviting some people of your age who I think it would be nice for you to meet.'

She laughed. 'I'm quite excited myself.'

Even with her new-found confidence, Alison was awestruck. All this for her. Because she was Mrs Considine's

111

second chance. She was getting what the other Camilla had not.

But there was a question that she had to steel herself to ask.

'Where are Michael and Anne? I haven't seen them around.'

'I should imagine they're in London,' replied Mrs Considine. 'That's where they said they were going. I'm afraid they've left my employment.'

'Left! You mean they – they've gone for good?'

'They are perfectly happy. They were very pleased with the compensation I gave them.'

'But – '

Alison was, for a moment, quite stunned by the ruthlessness of it. But, after all, when she came to think of it, what else could Mrs Considine have done? Had she really been expecting anything else?

'It was them or you, Ca,' said Mrs Considine, watching her.

'Yes. Yes, I see that. They won't tell anybody, though, will they?'

'No. You have no need to worry about anything. Now just forget about Anne and Michael. Did you hide the bike, incidentally?'

'In the storeroom at the back of the garage.'

'Good. Then why not go and choose some music for your party?'

Michael and Anne were sitting on the grass in Hyde Park, watching the boats on the Serpentine.

'I'm still recovering,' said Anne, 'are you?'

'I'm not sure I'm ever going to,' said Michael with a wry grin. He plucked a blade of grass and put the end in his mouth. 'Whoever would have thought she'd turn on us like that. It shook me rigid.'

'Still,' he said, after chewing reflectively for a little while, 'it's got its compensations. We've never been so rich.'

'The main thing, though,' said Anne, 'is that we've ended that business with the girl. We couldn't let that

112

go on, whatever happened. And it must be over or Mrs Considine wouldn't be in such a fury.'

'Oh, it's over all right,' said Michael. 'No doubt about that.'

Mrs Considine had given the Housmans no hint that Alison had betrayed them. She had merely told them that Alison had decided she was never coming to Rose-wilder again and accused them, in no uncertain terms, of being behind it, storming and raging at them till they confessed. Then she had screamed at them that they had ruined everything, that she would never see Alison again and that they must get out of her house at once. She had been very convincing.

'I don't regret what we did for a minute,' said Anne.

'Nor me,' said Michael. 'Oh, we just had to break that up.'

Alison spent some of the afternoon lolling on the sofa in the drawing room listening to records. This was the very height of luxury. At Holtwood Lane there had never been anything to play records on, but now she had the most expensive equipment and Camilla Considine's collection at her disposal.

Camilla's taste had apparently covered the whole field from classical to pop. Alison liked best the ballet music and the more tuneful of the popular songs and some of the lighter classics. There were plenty of those. She opened the french windows wide to let the music flood out on to the lawns.

When she had made her selection for the evening she went for a little walk down to the lake shore. It was, if anything, even hotter and more sultry than it had been earlier and, as she had anticipated, there was not a sail out on Codgerley.

The dinghy was on its launching trolley in the boat-house, beside the canoe. Alison realized that she wouldn't have Anne to sail with now. But perhaps soon there'd be other people? At the moment the future was unforeseeable.

After tea, which they had in the kitchen, Mrs Considine

took her upstairs to choose a dress for the party. This was, said Mrs Considine, 'to be no sloppy jeans and flip-flops affair'. Apparently she had asked everyone to dress up.

Alison found going through the wardrobe together thoroughly enjoyable, but it did occur to her that Mrs Considine always seemed to get a great deal of pleasure out of dressing her up, almost as if she were a doll. It didn't, however, strike her that this was the first time a thought critical of Mrs Considine, even of the mildest, had entered her mind. They chose an ivory coloured dress.

Shortly afterwards, another van arrived, this one from the contract caterers. It contained the manager, a girl assistant and apparently unlimited quantities of gateaux and apple juice and delicacies of every description.

At six o'clock, with Mrs Considine beside her for support, Alison prepared to receive her guests. They stood together by the window to watch the first one arrive. She was totally unknown to Alison, a bustling girl with that look of total self-possession which Alison had always hated and envied so much. She was getting out of a large car, through the windscreen of which an indulgent father-face could be glimpsed. Alison wondered where on earth Mrs Considine had produced her from.

'I telephoned some of the better families in the area,' said Mrs Considine with a smile, as if answering Alison's unspoken question, 'and said that now my daughter was home I would like her to meet some boys and girls of her own age. Everyone seemed pleased to be invited . . .

'Incidentally, Ca, I've told everyone that the party is to celebrate your coming home from Switzerland for good. If anybody asks you about the school, say you don't want to talk about it. You hated it too much.'

Even if Alison had wanted to object it would have been too late. The doorbell was ringing. But anyway she didn't.

'Supposing anybody asks me if I know Alison Allbright?' she said, remembering Raine's question.

'Tell them the truth. Tell them that I got to know her because my chauffeur ran over her bicycle. That I befriended her and took her to Italy for a holiday. But then you came back and . . .'

'We didn't get on?'

'Exactly.'

It was what Alison had told her family.

The guests were arriving thick and fast. A succession of faces, some of which Alison knew and some of which she didn't, all eager and smiling and pleased to meet her.

She got a thrill out of greeting Jill Mackenzie who, although older than most of the others, seemed delighted and grateful to have been invited. Alison would try to see that she won some nice prizes.

The face that she was really waiting for, of course, was Raine's.

At her home, they were just about to have tea.

'Where's Alison?' asked Keith.

'She's gone swimming with her friend, Raine,' replied Mrs Allbright. 'She said she might go back to their house.'

'Swimming? With Raine Lawlor?'

'Yes, why?'

'Raine Lawlor's been in town with her mother all afternoon. Buying clothes by the look of it. I saw her in Morley and Gilbert's when I was on my way to the library and she was just going into Taylor's when I came back.'

Alison's parents looked at each other.

'She's been lying again,' said Mr Allbright.

14
The Party

It was an evening of magic. Alison had never been to a party like this before. Though, when she came to think of it, she had never been to a party at all since – since when? Someone's birthday when she had been in the Infants' School?

The whole thing was quite expertly stage-managed by Mrs Considine. She must have spent the whole week planning and preparing. There was a hilarious treasure hunt and the treasure, when found, turned out to be a necklace of real, semi-precious stones. Other prizes were equally valuable. The magician proved to be not some mere local conjuror, but a being worthy of the name who materialized unexpectedly on the lawn in a puff of smoke to the accompaniment of much shrieking and hilarity. Also startling, and very beautiful, were the fireworks, the showers of golden rain and arching rockets that were suddenly let off as the sun sank low.

Most magical of all to Alison, however, was the fact that she was laughing and shrieking with everyone else, not just as one of them but as the most important, the one they were all looking up to. Thanks to Mrs Considine the other Alison Allbright, the one who was spontaneous and witty and fun, had emerged and become Camilla Considine . . .

And there was the fact, too, that she was with Raine.

Two highlights stood out during the early part of the evening. The first was when Raine arrived in her mother's car, looking shy and grateful when Alison went forward to greet her, picking her out from other arrivals (one of whom, Alison noticed, was Stephen Kirkpatrick on his bike and wearing the same trousers he wore to school). They were almost inseparable for the rest of the evening.

The second was a cruel triumph. Alison had been into the house to put some more records on, leaving Raine chatting to Mrs Considine in the garden. As she was about to return to them she saw two people get out of a car and then stand by it uncertainly as if not sure what to do. One of them was Susannah Strickland. She was wearing a stunning red dress. The other was presumably her mother.

Alison, brimming with confidence, walked over to them.

'I'm sorry,' she said, with deliberate cool suspicion, 'but I don't think I know you. Are you invited?'

'Well, I – ' began the embarrassed Mrs Strickland, ' – I think Susannah is – '

'You mean you're not sure?' Alison inquired in her plummiest voice.

'Your mother was inviting everyone else,' said Susannah lamely. 'She didn't actually ask me but I thought it must have been an oversight.'

'It wasn't,' said Alison. 'We can't have more than a certain number.'

They got back in the car. As they drove out of the gates Alison could see that Susannah was talking vehemently to her mother and appeared to be in tears.

Bursting with joy, Alison went to find Raine. Mrs Considine had just left her.

'A girl just tried to gatecrash,' she told her. 'Somebody called Susan – or was it Susannah? I sent her away.'

'Oh – ' began Raine, looking alarmed.

'I didn't like the look of her, anyway,' said Alison. 'She looks a snob to me and I don't like snobs. Mummy didn't like the look of her either. That's why she didn't invite her in the first place.'

Raine subsided. She was a little bit thoughtful and abstracted for a while after that, but then she cheered up again.

Alison's father was trying to thumb a lift. He had been lucky at first and got one very quickly along the Ardington

Road. The van driver had dropped him at the turn-off that led to Rosewilder. Now, however, his luck had run out.

Mr Allbright didn't know exactly where Rosewilder was, but he had gathered from what Alison had said after her first visit that it was somewhere along here and he was determined to find it. He was going to have a row with this woman who had turned Alison into a cunning, lying little snob. Alison had always had her faults, but she had had her good points, too. Where were they now? He was going to yank her out of that house once and for all. She *must* have gone there.

But he didn't have a car or even a bicycle. And there seemed to be no traffic on this little road. He had only seen one car on it and that coming towards him right at the very beginning of it.

It had in fact been the Stricklands returning chagrined from Rosewilder. He had just missed the surge of traffic to and from the party.

As a young man he would have thought nothing of walking the whole way there and very quickly, too. But his wretched rheumatism made it very hard now.

Alison and Raine sat together by the lake shore. They had brought a picnic and were sharing the same plate. From the lawns they could hear shrieks and laughter.

'It's heavenly, isn't it, said Raine. She was watching the lake and some mallard drifting across it. 'I've never seen Codgerley from this side before. There's something quite primeval about it, especially in this heat. I could easily believe there were savage tribes roaming around on the other side, among the trees.'

Although it was evening it was still hot.

'You're so lucky to live in a place like this,' said Raine.

They were totally relaxed together now. Alison had lost any fear that Raine might realize who she really was. And Raine had got over her initial shyness and wonder at being singled out for friendship by the hitherto remote, almost legendary Camilla Considine.

Alison did not now feel the slightest tremor when Raine

smiled and said suddenly, 'You were being cagey about Alison, then. You *did* meet her and you didn't like her.'

Alison turned her face away and looked at the ducks floating on Codgerley.

'Who told you?'

'Your mother. It's amazing. What a dark horse Alison is! Your mother told me all about it. How she had Alison out here two or three times and took her to Italy. Alison's never let on you know. She was even at Bransome Park when the rest of us were at a concert there. She's a funny girl.'

'Is she a friend of yours?' asked Alison carefully.

'She was my friend,' Raine said.

There was a pause. Alison wasn't sure she ought to go on with this. Perhaps she ought to bring the subject to a close. But it was irresistible.

'But she isn't any longer? Why?'

Raine seemed reluctant to reply. 'Oh, I dunno. It was just impossible.' She threw a piece of roll towards the ducks but they flapped and scuttled away from it.

'Then you don't mind that I didn't like her?'

Raine laughed shortly. 'I wondered if you'd been cagey in case it would offend me. No, of course I don't mind. Nobody else likes her, so why should you?'

That was a shock. Even if she'd known it, it was still a shock.

'But you must have liked her,' said Alison, summoning up her courage from the depths, 'you were friends.'

'I think I must be a freak,' said Raine, wryly.

Alison continued to stare at the lake. She could feel her face quivering.

'Why was it impossible?' she persisted.

'Oh, she just never gave anything,' said Raine. 'It was such hard work being friends with her. I always had to make the running, invite her to things, make the first move. While she was so prickly all the time, looking for slights. It was as if I had to keep on proving to her all the time that I really was her friend. It wore me down till I couldn't take any more.'

'Maybe things are difficult for her,' said Alison tightly.

'Maybe. She never even took me home. I thought per-

119

haps she was ashamed of it or that she had grumpy parents. I did see her once going in through the gate of quite a nice house, but afterwards I thought about it and it didn't seem like Alison. Maybe she lives in some cottage in the grounds. With Alison you just never know.'

'Well, there you are,' said Alison. 'You can't really know how difficult things might be for her.'

Raine said in a hard voice: 'I think perhaps they are. But the real trouble with Alison is that she's totally selfish.'

That was another shock. Like a punch. She ought not to go on with this but she had to. Anyway, Raine was in full flow now.

'Look at the way she treats her brother, for instance. She's got this younger brother, Keith. He's in the next form down at school. He's a nice boy but very quiet and shy and nothing to look at – bit round-shouldered – and he'd have loved a helping hand from Alison when he first came to Sturridge High. But she's always ignored him. It's as if he's a hole in the air, as if he doesn't *exist*.'

'What do you think she should do?' said Alison.

'Well, not *ignore* him, just because he doesn't fit in with some fine idea that Alison's got about herself. Mind you, I think Keith'll have the last laugh. He doesn't waste time mooching around feeling sorry for himself, like Alison. He gets on with things. Keith'll finish up at Oxford or Cambridge if you ask me.'

It was one shock after another now. It was also coming as an unnerving revelation to Alison that Raine had been so observant. She hadn't realized that Raine was even conscious of Keith's existence.

'Alison never even noticed the way other people stopped bothering with me so much while I was friendly with her. If she had done it would only have pleased her, she's so possessive and jealous. But nobody likes her very much and it made them sort of suspicious of me. Susannah Strickland used to get very indignant with me.'

'Susannah Strickland?'

'That's the girl you said tried to gatecrash. I'm sure she wasn't really gatecrashing, by the way. It was a misunderstanding. But she used to get really worked up about Alison, especially about the way she treated her brother. She said a girl like that couldn't be worth knowing. Susannah's very sweet.'

For Alison it was as if a secret door had suddenly been opened, giving a new view into a room she had lived in for a long time. The room now looked back-to-front and topsy-turvy.

'Didn't you say anything to Alison?' she asked.

'You can't,' said Raine. 'She's too prickly.' She looked at Alison. 'For someone who didn't like her, you sound quite sympathetic towards her.'

Alison realized that she had come dangerously close to being indiscreet. She shrugged.

'I suppose,' she said, 'I was thinking that it's all very well for – well, for me and this Susannah girl to say we don't like her, but she may have to face all sorts of things we know nothing about.'

'Maybe,' said Raine. 'But if she does, I expect her brother does, too, and he hasn't become selfish. Anyway, in a way I sort of envy the Allbrights.'

'Envy?' said Alison.

'Well, don't laugh, but in a way I always think they're more genuine than some of the rest of us at school. More rough edges but more truly alive. I can just see Keith Allbright being a big noise some day and he'll love every minute of it because he's slogged there by himself without any fond parents smoothing the way. The Allbrights don't seem to have fond parents. You never see them hanging around the school interfering and looking after their little darlings' interests, like nearly everybody else's. Mine for instance – '

'And what about Alison? How do you see her in a few years' time?'

'I don't know. Alison's very intelligent, actually, but it all seems to run to waste somehow.'

'You don't envy her, then. Only her brother.'

'I know it sounds stupid but I could do, easily. In a way it's boring being one of the people whose parents have money, always being looked after and never any challenges. Like me, up to a point, though my parents don't have that much –' She gave an embarrassed laugh. 'I'm sorry, Ca. Your mother has. I wasn't meaning –'

'I know,' said Alison. 'But not many would agree with you.'

'The trouble is,' said Raine, 'that when I'm with you it's just like being with Alison in some ways. You're so like her but so much nicer. Alison without the hang-ups . . .

'I'm making her sound terrible, aren't I? But I still like her. It's a pity she's so impossible. I sometimes feel guilty when I see her wandering around by herself at school, or think of her sitting at home alone. But there's nothing I can do.'

'Like some apple juice?' asked Alison. 'I'll go and get you some.'

She wanted to be by herself to adjust her mind to the new, brutal picture of Alison Allbright that had just been presented to her. Raine might still harbour a liking for Alison Allbright and think she was 'truly alive', but she, Alison, didn't. She didn't want ever to know anything about her again.

As she walked on to the lawn she saw that Mrs Considine was standing nearby, looking towards the front of the house. A wave of gratitude swept over her. This was the person who had rescued her from being Alison Allbright. She wanted to identify with her.

'Hallo, Mummy,' she said.

Then she saw what Mrs Considine was looking at. Mr Allbright was standing by the corner of the house, dazedly surveying the proceedings.

He hadn't seen Alison yet but he was bound to at any moment.

15
Goodbye, Alison Allbright

Alison couldn't move. Then she saw that Mrs Considine had turned to her. She appeared quite unconcerned.

'He looks angry,' she said. 'What did you say to him before you came here today?'

'I didn't tell him I was coming here. I said I was going swimming at Codgerley with Raine Lawlor and going to her house afterwards. I said I wasn't coming here any more because Camilla had come back and we didn't get on.'

'Very well. I'll attend to it. I think it's time this was cleared up anyway. Where are you on your way to?'

'To get some apple juice.'

'Then carry on. There's no need for you to be concerned. I'm glad he's come.'

Mrs Considine strolled towards Alison's father.

Alison moved towards the tables. She wasn't altogether sure what Mrs Considine meant about 'time this was cleared up', and on the whole she didn't want to know. Mrs Considine would know best what to do.

She was trembling with nerves, though. The girl from the catering firm had to get some more bottles of apple juice from a crate and while she was doing so, Alison was left standing by the table. She saw Mrs Considine join her father and begin to talk with her usual charm. Her father was responding angrily. How, she wondered, had he found out about her coming here?

Then, to her horror, Alison saw that Mrs Considine, while continuing to talk volubly, was pointing towards her. Her father was glancing round.

For a moment they were looking straight at each other across the lawns.

'Your apple juice,' said the girl and Alison unfroze, almost knocking some bottles over in her agitation. She picked up the glasses and, not daring to look again towards her father in case he was striding towards her, she started to walk back towards the lake. Then she risked a glance.

He was going! Turning sheepishly away!

Alison halted. What had Mrs Considine said to him?

For a moment she was tempted to run after him. He was walking stiffly because of his rheumatism and he looked uncouth and utterly out of place in this glamorous setting. How had he got there? Was he going to walk back?

The temptation did not last. She didn't want to be Alison Allbright again, the girl nobody liked. As he went out of the gates, Mrs Considine arrived by her side.

'I think I should have one of those apple juices to celebrate,' she said with a smile and took one from Alison's hand. She raised the glass. 'To us, the Considines,' she said and drank.

'What did he say?' asked Alison, bewildered.

'It seems that his son saw Raine Lawlor in town this afternoon. I simply told him that Raine Lawlor was here, but his daughter wasn't. And that just because his daughter told a lie about going swimming with Raine Lawlor, that didn't mean that she didn't go swimming at all. She probably did, perhaps alone or perhaps she met up with some other friend . . .'

'But when you pointed at me?'

'I was simply pointing out *my* daughter. Telling him how they don't get on together. How they're so alike in appearance but so dissimilar in every other way . . .'

Mrs Considine was smiling her odd smile. Alison stared at her.

'But – but what am I going to do when I go back? What am I going to say?'

She stopped because Mrs Considine was laughing.

'Oh, Ca, Ca, haven't you realized yet? You're not going back.'

She handed the glass back.

'You'll have to get another apple juice, Ca, but before you do that I'd like you to do something for me. I'd like you to get your bicycle, your swimming costume and towel and the clothes you came in and put them in the back of my car. Without anyone seeing.'

'In – in the back of your car?'

'Yes, Ca. There is no need to repeat things. This is not a military establishment. Just do it quickly.'

A few minutes later, Mrs Considine drove away from Rosewilder very fast. When she got to the top road, she turned left in the opposite direction to Sturridge Minster.

Alison, meanwhile, was rejoining Raine.

'You seem to have been away a long time,' said Raine. 'I've been sitting here dreaming.'

'I've been talking to – to my mother,' replied Alison.

She was in a total daze.

Mrs Considine drove towards the setting sun. She was following the north shore of Codgerley. After a time she left the lake behind, then forked left to Ardington.

In Ardington town centre she turned left again, following the sign to Sturridge Minster. This brought her back to the south side of the lake, but from the opposite direction to the way Alison normally approached it.

When she was nearly at the spot where the barbecue had been held she stopped and reversed into the entrance to a lane, then got out of the car and went down to the barbecue site on foot. She could hear thunder growling in the distance. A breeze had sprung up suddenly and black clouds were starting to darken the sky.

Having made sure that the place was deserted she brought Alison's belongings from the car. She placed the bicycle in a not-too-obvious spot among some bushes and laid the clothes, wrapped in the towel, beside it.

The swimming suit she would take back to Rosewilder with her. That could be burnt.

As she drove back to Rosewilder the way she had come, lightning flickered and some heavy drops of rain splashed on the windscreen. She put her foot down a little further. The catering manager had been happy to take c arge of the party while she nipped out but she didn't want to be away too long, especially as there was a storm coming.

Mr Allbright was still walking. He was bewildered and frightened. Not a single car had passed him since leaving Rosewilder and the signs were that he was going to be caught in a downpour. But it wasn't that that was worrying him. It was Alison. Where was she? Why had she lied?

He was kicking himself now for not being more pushing with Mrs Considine. Why hadn't he asked her if she'd drive him round to the other side of the lake to see if Alison was there? Or even if she'd let him telephone the police?

He did wonder whether he ought not to turn round now and go back there and ask her if he could do that. But no. Apart from feeling weary, he was too worried about making a still bigger fool of himself than he had already.

Alison was probably at home. She had probably walked in the door five minutes after he'd left. He was getting in a stew about nothing. He'd already had the wind taken out of his sails once, storming up to Rosewilder to have a row with Mrs Considine only to come away with his tail between his legs. He had been entirely wrong in jumping to conclusions that Alison had gone to Rosewilder.

That girl! She had looked like Alison but no wonder the two of them didn't get on. As if Alison ever *could* have got on with somebody like that. They weren't in the same world. How had Alison ever got mixed up with people like that in the first place? Why had she ever thought it would last?

It was starting to rain heavily. Two cars passed him before he came to the Ardington–Sturridge Minster Road but neither stopped.

When he arrived at the main road he paused in an agony of indecision. Should he turn left towards home or right towards Codgerley and the pier which was the most likely place Alison would have gone swimming?

He was weary and drenched and knew that he was going to pay for this in future pain. He was alternating between extreme anger at Alison for placing him in this predicament and frantic worry about her.

He tried to tell himself that he was getting it all out of proportion. He was worrying over nothing.

Nevertheless he turned right towards Codgerley. He'd be hating himself all the way home if he didn't check there first.

He did have a bit of luck after that. A farmer in a Range Rover stopped for him.

Another surge of traffic to and from Rosewilder was starting now, this time taking the guests home. He'd just missed that, too.

Alison was at the front door saying goodbye to Stephen Kirkpatrick who was fumbling to tell her sheepishly what a fantastic time he'd had. She had noticed him several times during the course of the party, sometimes joining eagerly in games, sometimes standing around almost open-mouthed at the splendour of it all. At least he hadn't appeared to be trying to pinch anything.

She had had several little day-dreams about how she would get her own back on him at the party, but when it came to the point it hadn't mattered enough. At school it had always been as if he were towering and important and she were looking up at him. Here he seemed clumsy and loutish and naïve and she seemed to be looking down. It was sufficient satisfaction to look down.

He dashed away through the rain and flickering light-ning to a waiting estate car. He'd managed to cadge a lift from someone, putting his bike in the back. There was a queue of people waiting to say goodbye to Alison and thank her, amongst them Jenny Allingham and others from school. She had totally forgotten now that there might be any reason for nervousness on her part. She was Camilla Considine and Alison Allbright was another person, some-one whom she desired to protect and avenge – but still another person. She had dismissed the memory of her father's visit from her mind.

Raine was the last to go. The two girls stood together under a big umbrella by Mrs Lawlor's car while she sat inside and raised her eyebrows to heaven in indulgent despair. 'You'll be soaked!' she cried out of the window but they didn't care. They swapped telephone numbers and chatted about the exciting things they might do together during the summer until Mrs Lawlor could stand it no longer and opened the door and virtually pulled Raine inside. Alison ran outside the gates so that she could wave goodbye till the last possible moment.

When she went inside there was music playing and Mrs Considine was sitting on the sofa, one leg crossed over the other, arms extended along the back, smiling at her.

'They've all gone, Ca,' she said. 'Just the two of us left by ourselves. It was a good party, wasn't it?'

'It was wonderful.'

For a fraction of a second as she stood there the realization came to Alison that she had arrived at that high wall beyond which she had been unable to see.

'For a girl of your age,' said Mrs Considine, 'it seems high time you were in bed. You must be very tired, but perhaps you ought to have a bath first.'

Alison looked at her.

'I hope you didn't have any different plans in mind,' said Mrs Considine good-humouredly. She got up.

'There was a girl called Alison Allbright. She was no good to anybody, especially to herself. She doesn't exist any longer.'

Alison was still looking at her.

'Aren't you having a wonderful time, Ca? Can't you see an even more wonderful future ahead?'

Alison nodded.

'Just rely on me to see to everything, Ca. You don't have to worry about a thing. Now off to the bathroom.'

'All right,' said Alison.

She found pyjamas and dressing gown put out for her in the bathroom. She lay in the scented water and thought of the party, of the summer ahead, of Raine and of that beautiful bedroom which she was about to go to. After a while, Mrs Considine heard singing.

When Alison had gone to bed, Mrs Considine put a raincoat over her head and went out into the garden. It was still raining very heavily and lightning was persistently flickering in the distance beyond Codgerley. She wasn't absolutely sure but she thought that mixed up with the lightning she could see a pulsating bluish glow. It could have been the reflection of a light from a police car parked among the trees on the other side of the lake. Or perhaps more than one.

When Alison woke next morning it was to a sense of luxuriousness she had never known before, even during those glorious days in Italy. The storm had passed over during the night and sunshine was streaming through the gap in the curtains. She lay and looked at the pink and white bedroom and at the picture on the table beside her.

Soon after nine o'clock there was a knock at the door and Mrs Considine came in with some tea on a silver tray which she placed on the bedside table.

'I thought I'd spoil you a little,' she said. She went to the window and drew the curtains fully apart, then stood there gazing out.

Alison piled the pillows up behind her and leaned back contentedly, sipping her tea.

'What are you looking at?' she asked. 'Is it something special?'

'Come and look too,' said Mrs Considine.

Alison got out of bed and, taking her tea with her, went over and stood beside Mrs Considine. She couldn't see anything special.

'There are some boats on the lake already,' she said, peering.

'Frogmen,' said Mrs Considine. 'I had a look at them through the binoculars earlier. They're looking for Alison Allbright, but they won't find her. She's gone for ever.'

A cold feeling struck at Alison.

Mrs Considine turned away from the window. 'Come downstairs when you've finished your tea and we'll have some breakfast.'

She went out of the room and closed the door behind her, leaving Alison still by the window. Alison stood there recalling how Mrs Considine had taken her bike and clothes away last night. She hadn't let herself think about it deeply then.

Mrs Considine was in the kitchen making scrambled eggs when, some time later, Alison appeared fully dressed in the doorway. She turned around and looked at her with perhaps some apprehension.

'I'd like to make plans,' said Alison, her face glowing. 'All the summer's ahead and there are thousands of things I want to do. And I'd like Raine to come everywhere. Can I ring and ask her to come over today?'

Mrs Considine laughed and turned back to the scrambled eggs.

'You've been having a lot of excitement lately, Ca,' she said. 'I think we ought to have a quiet time now, just for a few days, just the two of us.'

'All right,' said Alison happily, 'anything you say.'

'There *are* plans to make,' said Mrs Considine, thoughtfully stirring the scrambled eggs. 'I must find a married couple to replace the Housmans – but not living in this time, I think. And we'll need a private tutor for you – now that you're back from Switzerland I don't really like the idea of your going away to a boarding school again. But there's no hurry. We'll just have a quiet time together for now.'

It dawned upon Alison that she wouldn't be going to Sturridge High ever again.

There were a few minutes before breakfast and Alison couldn't resist going out into the sunshine. The grass was still a little wet and she took her shoes off and twirled for joy on the lawn.

But she kept away from any place where she might see the lake.

In the late afternoon, Alison and Mrs Considine were having tea on the lawn when the garden bell of the telephone rang.

'I'll answer it in the kitchen and take these plates inside at the same time,' said Mrs Considine, getting up. 'Bring the cups when you come in.'

When Alison followed her with the cups a few minutes later she was still at the wall telephone extension in the kitchen. She sounded distressed. She was saying:

'I can't help feeling a little responsible. You remember I told you I took her to Italy with me – yes, I felt sorry for the girl, she didn't seem to have much fun and besides – yes, quite, she's – she was the image of Ca – but I rather think that after a week in the Mediterranean and using flippers and things she may have got the idea that she was a better swimmer than was really the case . . . yes, yes, I quite agree, it seems like over-confidence . . . look, Ca's just come in. I'll hand you over to her. What a dreadful shock this is!'

She pointed the receiver at Alison who was standing rigidly in the kitchen doorway. 'It's Raine.'

Alison took it and lifted it to her ear. 'Hallo,' she said nervously.

'Oh, Camilla, it's about Alison. It looks as if she's been drowned. In the lake. In Codgerley. The police have been there all day but they're giving up hope of even – even of finding her . . .'

Raine sounded distraught.

'It seems she went swimming there yesterday by herself and – and her father found her clothes and bike still there last night. Oh, Ca, I was talking about her, wasn't I . . .'

She was almost choking.

'Apparently a lot of the bottom of Codgerley is just terrible for finding anybody . . . it's all soft mud and weed and rubbish, you could get held down and never be found again . . . they're talking about putting up warning notices but it's a bit late now, isn't it? Too late for Alison . . .

'Oh, and Ca – Alison told her parents she was going swimming with *me*. A policewoman asked me if I'd seen her. Isn't it terrible? She hated letting anybody see that she was lonely. To say she was going with *me*!

'I really don't want to talk now, Ca. I just wanted to let you know . . . your mother's so concerned. She's talking about arranging a memorial service in the Minster.'

16
Alison's Revenge

On the following Friday, Alison went with Mrs Considine to the memorial service. She hadn't wanted to, of course, but Mrs Considine had been adamant, apparently feeling it necessary that Alison should see and hear for herself that the old Alison Allbright had really gone.

The only point that Mrs Considine was prepared to concede was that it might be painful for Mr and Mrs Allbright if they were to see Camilla Considine, who so much resembled their lost daughter, at the service. Therefore the two of them got to the Minster early and sat to one side and at the back where they could see but not easily be seen from the front pews where the family would be. It was a showery day, cool for June, and Alison wore an almost white raincoat with a dusky pink scarf around her head, tied under the chin. She felt quite detached, as though Alison Allbright were some remote memory. At the same time she was taut, nervous, watchful.

She was astonished by the beauty of the floral decorations in the Minster. Someone had been spending a fortune at the florist's and she guessed it was Mrs Considine. She knew that Mrs Considine had been the driving force behind the whole service, that she had telephoned the parents of some of the guests at the party and got them to obtain the consent of Mr and Mrs Allbright to make the necessary arrangements. Alison had shut her mind to it.

In any case, she had had too much else to occupy her thoughts – mainly the sheer joy of *being* Camilla Considine, though not entirely so. She had in fact been experiencing a few minor irritations. Mrs Considine had kept on a little about their having a quiet time together and had continued to discourage her from ringing Raine. She had previously seemed so anxious for Alison to meet other people, but now . . .

Also, Rosewilder was starting to go downhill a little. Mrs Considine had not yet replaced the Housmans and didn't seem to be in a great hurry to do so, and the house and grounds were far too big to keep clean and tidy without help. Nor had she made any moves about a tutor.

However, Alison realized that this was all quite understandable in the circumstances and that she mustn't be impatient.

She sat and watched the Minster filling up.

And it *was* filling up. It was quite extraordinary. She had expected that very few people would come and those only because Mrs Considine had organized them into it. But people were pouring in. Just about the whole school seemed to be coming, masters and mistresses as well as pupils. That was Mr Craig, looking very solemn in a dark blue suit. And Mrs Shearing! And there was Mr Shaw, the Headmaster! He was walking towards the front pews preceded by Mrs Shaw. Alison was amazed that he even knew about her.

All these people just for that unnoticeable and unnecessary nobody, Alison Allbright! None of them had even given her a second glance in the past . . .

Susannah Strickland was coming in with her parents. *Susannah Strickland*! Having the nerve to look all poker-faced!

Someone in the front row was standing up and looking round, eyes searching every corner of the Minster. Raine.

She had seen Alison, was coming towards her.

'Hallo, Mrs Considine. Hallo, Ca,' she said. 'Isn't it a terrible thing to happen?' She looked very strained. 'I hoped you'd be here.'

'Are your parents coming?' Mrs Considine asked her. 'I can't see your mother.'

'They've gone to pick up Alison's parents and brother. The Allbrights don't have a car. They're late though. It's a minute to three and they haven't arrived yet.'

Raine's parents at Alison's home! Alison tried to imagine it . . .

'I must say,' said Raine, 'it's amazing the way so many people have rallied around Mr and Mrs Allbright. Nobody knew where they lived at first because Alison never let on, but I got Keith to take me there. And since then lots of people have been to see them – '

She glanced round, hearing more people enter the Minster. Her parents and the Allbrights weren't among them but Stephen Kirkpatrick was.

'You see that boy over there – Stephen Kirkpatrick, he was at your party – he's been there a lot. You'd never think so to look at him, would you, but it seems he went round with some flowers first of all. I know because Susannah was at the Allbrights when he called, and when he saw her he got embarrassed and nearly squashed them trying to hide them behind his back. I think he used to tease Alison quite a bit at school. Perhaps it's on his conscience – no, that's mean – I think maybe he's quite nice. Oh, dear! Isn't it strange and horrible to be talking about Alison like this?'

The last words were spoken in an increasingly high-pitched voice and Raine's face seemed to be on the verge of crumpling, but then she steadied herself. Mrs Considine watched her sympathetically.

'Sorry about that,' she said. 'What was I saying? About visiting the Allbrights. Susannah's been there a lot, too. Mrs Allbright told her that it comforted her to see Alison's friends – said Alison had never introduced her to any and it was nice to meet them now . . . so Susannah's been encouraging lots of people to go along. They've been saying they were Alison's friends.'

She glanced at her watch with a frown. 'It's gone three! Where are they, I wonder?'

'There are your parents now, Raine,' said Mrs Considine. 'They've just come in.'

Alison looked round. Standing just inside the entrance to the Minster, in hurried conversation with the Vicar who had greeted them, were Mr and Mrs Lawlor. And beside them, in his school uniform, was Keith.

'But where are Alison's parents?' said Raine. 'Just a minute, I'm going to find out.'

She hurried off. Alison watched as she had a few words with her mother. Then she returned briefly to whisper:

'At the last minute they said they wouldn't come. Couldn't face it. So Keith came alone. Oh, isn't the whole thing terrible? I'd better go and join my parents now.'

When Raine had gone, Alison realized that she was beginning to feel much better, more relaxed. She hadn't admitted it to herself, but it had been the prospect of seeing her parents again which had made her feel taut and nervous. It was an enormous relief that they weren't coming.

She was also recovering from hearing about how all those people from school had gone trooping along to Holtwood Lane to talk to her parents.

She had always gone to such lengths to keep her home life secret from everybody because of the fear of being looked down on. And yet it had now been laid bare, exposed to everyone's gaze. It was a thought that took some getting used to.

But one thing she could appreciate. Revenge. Even Stephen Kirkpatrick had some sort of conscience, then. Flowers! She hoped they'd cost him a lot. She hoped he'd be sorry for evermore for the way he'd made her life a misery. She hoped Susannah was suffering, too. Now that her parents weren't coming, she was all set to savour this service.

There was much for Alison to savour, in particular the address by Mr Craig who explained that he was giving it, rather than Mr Shaw, because as her form master he had been closer to Alison Allbright than any other member of the school staff.

'However,' he said solemnly and deliberately, giving each word weight, 'I have to confess that I wasn't *very* close.'

'You weren't within a hundred miles,' thought Alison in the pause that followed. She felt utterly detached from the proceedings. She gazed at the vaulting above her and, with her forefinger, pushed the lapel of her raincoat up against her cheek while resting her elbow on her other hand. It was an attitude which made her feel very glamorous and sophisticated. She wondered how long Mr Craig had had that suit. It was too tight for him and made him look seedy.

He was continuing, eyes downcast, hands on the sides of the lectern.

'Alison was a quiet and solitary girl. She had few friends for she was not easy to get to know, though I am sure that many of you tried . . .'

'No,' thought Alison, 'no they didn't actually, not if we're really honest about it.'

'We can't say of Alison that she left behind her a record of great achievement. It would be dishonest to pretend that. She didn't shine either academically or on the sports field.'

'Usually came around the bottom of the class,' thought Alison. 'And always on the other side of the field from where the action was, just trailing around after the others, hoping the ball wouldn't come too near, scared she'd make a mess of it . . .'

'But she has left us with something much more profound and, I hope, lasting. I think I am not alone in feeling that. I think it is why there are so many of us here today.'

His hands tightened on the lectern. He crouched forward a little.

'It is a terrible thing to have been left with. It is the feeling that I ought to have tried harder with Alison. Even more terrible because there can be no second chance. I think that throughout my life I shall never be able to forget that I did not try hard enough.

'These feelings have come only because she has been lost to us. Don't ever let's make the same mistake again. Let's make sure we try harder with others who are lonely and shy as she was, in future. Let that be Alison's legacy to us.'

He paused and looked down at the floor in front. When he spoke again it was very quietly.

'I would give much to have a second chance with Alison Allbright.'

From somewhere came a sob. Elsewhere the sound of a

nose being blown. Alison smiled at the vaulting. Revenge was sweet.

Just before the end of the service, Mrs Considine rose quietly and touched Alison on the sleeve to indicate that they should go. Alison had been hoping to stay behind for a few minutes for a chat with Raine but nevertheless she got up obediently.

The only person to see them leave was Keith. Unknown to Alison he had glanced round at her several times during the service.

'I was hoping to have a few words with Raine,' said Alison as she and Mrs Considine got into the car.

'Oh, there's plenty of time for that,' replied Mrs Considine. She seemed thoughtful. 'It's a pity that Mr and Mrs Allbright didn't come to the service after all.'

Alison wasn't really listening. She was in a state of elation at having got through the service and actually feeling better for it. And at having finally got rid of Alison Allbright.

Mrs Considine remained thoughtful all the way back. It was as if she knew that something had been left out of the bewitching process, perhaps something crucial.

'I was thinking today,' said Keith over tea, 'supposing that girl isn't Mrs Considine's daughter at all! Supposing it's Alison all dressed up!'

'Don't be so cruel, Keith,' said his mother. 'That's a silly, silly thing to say, isn't it?' She was sitting staring into space, not eating.

'You ought to know better than to say things like that,' said Mr Allbright.

That evening, Mrs Considine became angry with Alison for the first time. Alison had again asked if she might ring Raine and again been reminded that they were still having a quiet time together. Then, at about eight o'clock, while they were in the sitting room, the telephone rang and Mrs Considine went into the hall to answer it, closing the door behind her.

Alison, who was still elated, wondered if it might be Raine and she couldn't resist getting up, opening the door and listening. She was just in time to hear Mrs Considine say:

'Yes, I'll tell her, Raine. And she will ring you sometime soon. It's just that she really does want to spend a little time quietly at home at present. Yes . . . yes . . . I will . . .'

'Is that Raine?' called Alison excitedly. 'Can I speak to her?'

She almost ran along the corridor and into the hall. When she got there Mrs Considine was standing with one hand on the receiver which was now back on its rest. She looked furious.

'Were you eavesdropping, Ca?' she shouted. 'Now for goodness' sake stop pestering me about Raine Lawlor. If you don't, I shall have to forbid you to see her again.'

Alison was shaken.

17
The Spell is Broken

Next morning, Mrs Considine apologized for losing her temper and was as charming as she had ever been. Nevertheless, things weren't to be the same again. Also, during the days that followed, Alison began to feel afraid

It was becoming clear to her that the 'quiet time together' was continually being extended. Probably Mrs Considine had every intention of replacing the Housmans, of finding a tutor, of allowing and encouraging Alison to lead a full and exciting life. But not yet . . . always not quite yet.

Alison was also beginning to feel cut off from the outside world. Rosewilder was several miles even from the nearest shop. It was all right having a Rolls-Royce in the garage, but if you couldn't drive it . . . She didn't even have a bicycle now.

Mrs Considine didn't go out anywhere, even to buy food. They were living out of the deep freeze.

During the first few days the telephone rang several times. Twice Alison eavesdropped cautiously. On each occasion the caller was apparently someone who had been at the party at Rosewilder and was now anxious to return the hospitality. To Alison's dismay, Mrs Considine refused both invitations on the grounds that Camilla was in need of rest and quiet. The phone calls became fewer and then stopped.

Alison was continually hoping that Raine would not have been put off by the cool reception she had received from Mrs Considine and would ring again. But if she did, would she get a better reception this time? Much as Alison longed to ring her, she didn't dare. It had become understood that she wasn't to use the telephone.

Although Raine was hardly mentioned, she was becoming a deeply felt issue between them.

They had their meals together and sunned themselves on the lawns. Alison fed and groomed Pippin, listened to records and helped Mrs Considine cook and weed the garden. Sailing and riding held no appeal for her now. These things were no fun alone.

She also tried to help with the housework, though discouraged by Mrs Considine who seemed to feel it was beneath her. Mrs Considine herself was utterly incompetent at any form of housework and it was obvious that this was the first time in her life she had ever been confronted by any. Every labour-saving device was available but she was nervous of using any of them, seeming to feel that, say, the dishwasher would explode if she switched it on.

Each day the house and grounds were becoming more unkempt.

One evening, over dinner, looking out over Codgerley as they had on Alison's first visit to Rosewilder, Mrs Considine talked about her husband.

'Of course, you were only three when he left home, Ca,' she said. 'You won't be able to remember anything about him at all.'

Alison gathered that he had been a surgeon with a Harley Street practice and that they had lived in London, in Hampstead. Mrs Considine had been very wealthy in her own right and after they had separated she had gone to the country with Camilla. Rosewilder was the second house she had moved to. She liked it because it was so self-contained, a little world of its own.

One day, Alison was surprised to see that the big wooden front gates were closed. She had a sudden, irrational fear that they might be locked and went over to try them. The cast-iron handle did turn, however. She opened the gate just a fraction to make sure. As she closed it again she heard Mrs Considine call, 'Ca! Where are you going?'

Alison jumped and turned to see her standing at the corner of the house. 'Nowhere,' she said.

That evening, before going to bed, Alison picked up the portrait of Camilla.

'She's forgotten about the second chance, hasn't she?' she said to it. 'She's becoming just like she was before.'

She badly wanted to talk to Raine. She had found herself looking at the phone as at a friend. It was her one possible link with the outside world. But it never rang now.

It was nearly midsummer and still very light, even with the curtains drawn. After she had got into bed she lay on her side and continued to look at the picture. During the last few days she had begun to feel that she was in a prison and it frightened her. But at the same time, in fact, ever since Mrs Considine's outburst over Raine, an even deeper fear had been growing gradually in her mind. Now she admitted to herself what it was.

How could anyone know that Mrs Considine's version of how the first Camilla had met her death was the true one? She knew now that Mrs Considine had a violent temper when crossed. And didn't they have fences or walls on Swiss mountain roads? All right, not everywhere perhaps and yes fences and walls could be in need of repair, but even so . . .

Like the fear of the gate being locked, it was irrational. But it was there.

However, it wouldn't have occurred to Alison to try to run away from Rosewilder. Where on earth could she run to? She *was* Camilla now.

She just wanted to talk to Raine.

About ten days after the memorial service during the school dinner break, Raine was leaving the building to join her friends when she heard her name called. Keith was standing, shy and hunched, outside the doorway.

Like others at Sturridge High, Raine had been at pains to be especially nice to Keith ever since Alison's disappearance, but she hadn't found it easy. Keith didn't adapt easily to being the centre of attention. She was pleased, therefore, to see him apparently being friendly.

'Yes?' she said.

'Have you got a few minutes? It's about Alison.'

'About Alison?' she repeated, her voice softening. 'What about her?'

'I don't think Alison drowned at all.'

She stared at him.

'I've tried to tell that to Mum and Dad but they just shut me up. I wanted to know what you think. You were friends with her.'

'But – I mean what are you saying? Where is she, then?'

'I think she calls herself Camilla Considine now. I think that was her in the Minster.'

'Come on,' said Raine, 'let's walk round the grounds while you tell me.'

Susannah and the others saw the pair of them deep in conversation and called to her, but Raine didn't hear.

'But I mean, *why* do you think that? It's so fantastic. You must have a reason before you can think a thing like that. Something solid.'

'She gave me the creeps,' was all Keith would say. 'She was after something. Mum and Dad were impressed because she went to school with titled people, but to me that doesn't mean a thing. I think it was Alison she was after.'

'But she can't be Camilla Considine,' said Raine, helplessly. 'Camilla Considine is – Camilla Considine. Oh, look – I'll tell my parents – maybe get them to ring Mrs Considine. But I can't do more than that, can I?'

Thinking about it during the afternoon, she decided that even that small promise was too much. He was being imbecilic, refusing to accept the truth, poor kid. Even so, she couldn't get it out of her mind.

Of course, her parents ridiculed the idea. And her mother flatly refused to ring Mrs Considine. What was she supposed to say? 'Good evening, Mrs Considine. I just wanted to inquire – is Camilla your daughter or is she stolen property?'

Mr and Mrs Lawlor returned to watching the local news on television and Raine went out into the hall and sat down by the telephone. They were right, of course. They didn't have any reason for ringing Rosewilder. But *she* had.

Raine had been thinking a lot about Camilla Considine ever since she had telephoned her on the evening of the day of the memorial service and had been fobbed off by Mrs Considine. She hadn't known then whether she were getting the brush-off or not, but if she were it seemed rather odd. Both Camilla and Mrs Considine had been so friendly earlier in the day. The situation had puzzled her. Since then Camilla hadn't rung and she hadn't known whether to try again . . . but perhaps she ought to.

She picked up the telephone.

At Rosewilder, Alison was sitting in a deck chair on the lawn when the garden telephone bell jangled into life and made her start. It was the first time it had sounded for days.

She jumped to her feet and looked towards the house. She knew it would be Raine. It had to be.

The jangling stopped. It was being answered.

And suddenly Alison knew that she couldn't just stand there. If Raine were to be snubbed once more she might never ring again.

Alison didn't know what she was going to do as she ran to the house. She just ran. When she burst into the hall she expected to find Mrs Considine there. But she wasn't.

Either the call was over already or she was answering it in the kitchen. Which? Alison couldn't resist it. She picked up the hall receiver and listened.

' – bed early with a headache, Raine,' Mrs Considine was saying on the kitchen extension.

Raine's voice. Shyly expressing her sympathy.

'. . . awfully busy at present, Raine . . . might not be able to get in touch with you for some time . . . do so as soon as she's able . . .'

There was an edge to Mrs Considine's voice.

Alison stood there, listening dumbly. She wanted to cry out to Raine that it wasn't true, that she was here. But she couldn't find the courage, or even the will to defy Mrs Considine. She heard the kitchen receiver replaced and the dialling tone start to buzz. She didn't think to put her own

143

receiver back on its rest, simply stood there dazedly allowing it to dangle from her hand.

She knew for certain now that Mrs Considine wasn't going to allow her to see Raine again.

The thick carpets muffled the sound of Mrs Considine's quick footsteps as she came along the corridor. As she advanced into the hall she was shouting, 'How dare you listen in to my phone calls, Camilla!'

She knocked the receiver from Alison's hand and Alison sprang away like a frightened animal. She snatched the telephone, frenziedly yanking it.

The cable jerked away from the wall first, then the telephone parted from the cable. Mrs Considine hurled it into the corner of the hall where it cracked against the floor tiles. 'Raine!' she spat out.

Alison cowered, her back against the door. Her last, her only means of communication with the outside world had gone. It lay broken in front of her.

After putting the phone down, Raine had continued to sit in the hall. She felt oppressed by the call but this, she supposed wryly, was because getting the big brush-off could hardly be other than unwelcome and hurtful. There was something else bothering her, though, something she couldn't quite put her finger on. Was it that click she'd heard on the line? As if somebody had been listening in on an extension.

The telephone in front of her rang and she picked it up. She had hardly announced herself when an awkward voice shouted nervously, 'It's Keith Allbright. I wondered what your parents said.'

'Look, Keith,' she said, 'I think if we want to do anything we've got to do it ourselves. Have you got a bike?'

'Alison's.'

'Would you like to come to Rosewilder and scout around, maybe see if we can see Camilla?' She looked at her watch. 'It's too late tonight, I suppose . . . tomorrow night?'

'Please,' said Keith. 'Tonight.'

Alison was in her room to which she had been ordered by

Mrs Considine. She had been thankful to escape, but now she wished there were a lock on the door for she could hear Mrs Considine coming up the stairs and she was frightened.

She got behind a chair, gripping the back of it tightly, as if it might provide some defence. Mrs Considine halted outside the door.

'Camilla,' she called. 'Camilla, I'm sorry. Do you forgive me?'

Alison's hands slackened on the chair.

'Yes,' she called back, with difficulty. Her mouth was very dry and she was watching the door handle.

There was a silence. Then Mrs Considine's voice came again, sadly:

'We could have been all right if it hadn't been for that girl, Ca.'

Another silence. Alison heard the creak of the floorboards as she walked away.

Until that moment, in spite of everything, Alison had remained bewitched. Now, like a sandcastle sucked by the tide, the spell started to crumble, slide and collapse.

Mrs Considine was right. Raine had proved too powerful a rival for her. Perhaps, even so, the spell might have held. If Alison had seen her parents in the Minster and faced up to what she was doing then, things might have been different in one way or another . . .

But she hadn't. And now her mind was starting to take in the enormity of what she had done.

She didn't want to be Camilla Considine any more. She wanted to go home.

As she stood there, hands gripping the chair tightly again, she knew that Mrs Considine would never willingly let her go. The fear was growing in her mind that while she remained within her power there could only be one end. What had happened to the real Camilla would happen to her.

Suddenly too terrified for caution, she pulled open the bedroom door and fled down the stairs. She left the house by way of the boiler room and didn't stop running till she reached the great wooden gates. She grasped the iron ring and tried to turn it.

The gates were locked.

From there she raced to where the wrought iron gate to the paddock fitted snugly in its archway in the wall, but that was locked, too. There were no other gates in the high wall that surrounded Rosewilder. Only the boats offered a way of escape.

Panic-stricken now, Alison made for the boathouse. As she neared it she heard the clang of the door being lowered and, through the shrubbery, she glimpsed Mrs Considine as she snapped shut the padlock.

Alison fled back to her room. Rosewilder had become a prison.

18
Coming Back

She had to escape.

In jeans and jumper and sandals Alison sat by the window and watched the sun begin to set beyond Codgerley to her right. She had thought of how she ought to be able to get out of the grounds quite easily provided she could leave the house without being seen. She was waiting for twilight.

Running through her mind all the time now was the memory of what had happened to the real Camilla.

Not many days ago, seated in the Minster in her almost-white raincoat and her dusky pink headscarf, Alison had felt cool and sophisticated and grown-up. Now she felt like a terrified little girl and she wanted her parents.

Mrs Considine was back in the house. She had come upstairs and called to Alison, asking her if she were all right and if she would like to come downstairs and have a hot drink.

Alison had replied that she had gone to bed. Then, after thankfully listening to the retreating footsteps, she had tried to think out as calmly as possible what to do. She must try to keep her wits about her as she had done with Michael Housman.

The gates were locked. The boats were shut away except for a cabin cruiser with neither sail nor fuel aboard.

However, there was one way of escape that Mrs Considine couldn't cut off – Codgerley. The walls to the grounds ended in the waters of the lake itself, at massive buttresses. Surely it would be quite easy to wade round one of these buttresses and get out of the grounds that way. She would get a bit wet and muddy, that was all.

All she was waiting for was twilight . . . She didn't want it to be too dark as she'd have to find her way first round the buttress, then back to Sturridge Minster. But she wanted enough shadow to allow her to remain inconspicuous if Mrs Considine should happen to look out of the window.

When the light had faded sufficiently she got up. Before going out of the room she picked up the portrait of Camilla. This girl had been a hated rival, a friend, and then one with her. Now Alison understood the unsmiling expression on her face. She laid the picture against her cheek for a moment. 'Goodbye,' she said, then she left the room.

Getting out of the house proved easy. She left by the quickest route, the front door, then ran, compulsively crouching, across the lawns. The lights were on in the drawing room. Mrs Considine must be in there.

In the shelter of the trees she paused for breath, then turned left and made for the wall which she followed down to the lake shore. Putting her left hand against the wall to steady herself she waded straight in. The water was extremely shallow, only inches deep. It was tepid. This was easy –

Her left leg sank deep into mud and seemed to be about to continue downwards for ever. In a panicky movement she hauled it partly out, staggered and found the other one going in. Threshing wildly, she flung herself round and down and grabbed at a tussock of grass by the lake edge. She wriggled her way out on her stomach and lay there gasping, her clothes oozing black mud.

If it were the same at the other wall, she could see now why Mrs Considine felt that Rosewilder was secure. Her jeans flapped solidly and coldly against her legs as she ran there.

It *was* the same. Too shallow for swimming and a bottom of near-liquid mud. Her plan had been a non-starter. Like a frightened rabbit now, she ran back to the jetty. Was there *anything* she could do? Any way of reaching that remote world she could see beyond Codgerley?

The bottom here, by the jetty, was firm, of course. She

knew that from pushing the dinghy out with Anne Housman. It was also deep enough to swim in. Anne had shown her that the deeper water formed a winding channel running out towards the islands in the middle and the opposite shore. But there was no hope of her swimming that far.

Would it be possible to swim out a little way then turn to the nearer shore? Who could tell?

Despairing, she had a sudden wild thought. She waded straight into the water. It was slimy underfoot but here there was solidity under the thin layer of mud. The water, still tepid even near the bottom, climbed to her knees, to her waist, almost to her armpits. Instinctively she stretched up, lifting her chin, and kept on going.

The water wasn't climbing higher! She was past the end of the jetty and the bottom had levelled out. Of course it might get deeper in parts but would it be possible to *walk* across Codgerley? Or part-walk, part-swim?

Far across Codgerley, a car's headlights tantalizingly swept along the road behind the barbecue site. It was rapidly getting darker.

She remembered what Raine had said. 'It's all soft mud and weeds and rubbish . . . you could get held down there and never be found again . . .'

In the stillness she heard a footstep ringing on the flagstone path in the garden behind her. She turned her head sharply. A tall shape, pale against the darkening trees, was emerging from the shrubbery. Alison tried to duck but too late.

'Ca!' screamed Mrs Considine. And then again, '*Ca!*'

It was a scream of rage and fear and fury.

Alison hurled herself at the water, threshing her way through it, half swimming, half trying to run.

When, exhausted, she paused to look back she saw that Mrs Considine had waded into the water too and was following her.

There was a nightmarish quality about the tall, elegant figure in a cream-coloured dress striding through the water. Her cry was still ringing in Alison's ears. She might well have given just such a shout of fury when Camilla Considine had jumped out of her car on that Swiss mountain road.

Alison turned and thrashed her way onwards, it hardly mattered in which direction. Sometimes the water was only waist high and the bottom was solid and the going was easy. Then the bottom would fall away and she would have to swim, splashing furiously. Or she would have to swim because the bottom had become mud. Or because weed was tangling her legs. The weed terrified her more than anything.

She was swallowing a lot of lake water. The taste of it filled her throat and she felt that if she had time she would be sick. But she didn't have time. Whenever she looked round, it was to see the tall pale figure striding or swimming behind her like some spirit of the lake. The race was fairly even. Mrs Considine, being so much taller and stronger, was able to stride more easily where the bottom allowed. But Alison, though herself a weak swimmer, was better than she was.

Nevertheless, Mrs Considine gained steadily. And Alison feared that at any moment she must strike a stretch of deep water or soft mud that it would be beyond her endurance to cross . . .

It was dark now. Instinctively, she had been heading for the directly opposite shore because that was where the road was and where she could see the car headlights blinking as they disappeared and reappeared among the trees. They looked as far away as ever.

It seemed now to be getting still darker and the car headlights were hardly appearing at all. She was in a black world of mud and water. Dimly, she realized why. She was behind one of the islands and quite close to it. Then she must have come a long way . . .

She knew now that she had to get on the island and rest, if only for a moment. A few precious seconds out of the water. The water was shoulder high. As she ploughed onwards, however, it became rapidly more shallow till it was only waist high.

Then suddenly her feet went straight down into mud. She tried to drag the right foot out but she was exhausted and it only sent the left foot deeper in. She keeled to one side, the left side of her face resting on the water. She threshed with her arms, trying to swim out, choking and spitting. She knew there was no hope of getting out. She was still sinking. She closed her mouth tight and tried to keep her nose out of water.

A tall, weird figure covered in mud and draped with weed strode towards her, legs dragging stiffly like a Martian robot.

As Alison's nose went under, Mrs Considine seized her under the arms and started to haul her upwards towards the island. She herself was floundering on rubbery legs and at every step the mud tried to suck her in. She was tall and strong enough to resist. But only just.

'Camilla, you little idiot,' she said tenderly. She was weeping. 'Camilla, you could have drowned.'

They were out of the water and Alison was lying on grass. She tried to struggle up but could only manage to raise herself on to her elbows. Beside her, Mrs Considine crouched on hands and knees, still weeping, now in gusting, racking, exhausted sobs.

'I'm Alison,' she found the strength to screech. 'Not Camilla. Alison, Alison, Alison.'

From a little way above, among the trees on the highest point of the island, a light stabbed out and she was held in its beam.

'Alison!' came a voice sharp with fear and astonishment. 'Alison, is that you?'

It was Raine's voice. Alison could see her silhouette behind the lantern she was holding. Beside her was another silhouette. Keith.

Alison Allbright had come back from the dead, out of Codgerley, brought by Mrs Considine. For a long, long time, it seemed, the lamp held her steady in its beam. She slumped forward again, coughing and choking, and was sick.

She was barely conscious of what was happening. Raine was holding her and she could hear Keith's voice. He was saying something about the kiss of life but that wasn't necessary. Nobody even realized at first that Mrs Considine had gone.

Alison found out later that Mrs Considine was drowned in Codgerley that night. She was some way off the direct route back to Rosewilder, in deep water, when she was found and it was thought that she must have got lost in the darkness.

Alison was told the news by a policeman during the long, strange period after she had come back from the cottage hospital, when she stayed in her room refusing to come out. Afterwards she watched the trains from her window and thought deeply about Mrs Considine. She wondered what would happen to Rosewilder now and who would live there.

She also learned how Raine and Keith had come to be on the island. They had cycled to Rosewilder to find the gates locked and had then had the mad idea of trying to row across Codgerley in the Lees' dinghy to see if they could do any spying from that direction. But they had been unable to find the channels and had ended up on the island in the darkness, just in time to hear the commotion.

Afterwards, they had taken her back across the lake in the dinghy and Raine had cycled to the nearest phone box and rung her parents, who had themselves become quite worried by this time. It was they who had taken Alison to the hospital and broken the news to Mr and Mrs Allbright.

After their first reactions, Alison's parents seemed to her almost maddeningly uncensorious. They accepted her back with a sort of dumb, unquestioning, patient relief and gratitude. She herself fully realized how monstrous her behaviour had been, and would almost have preferred to be beaten.

'I'm sorry, Mum, I'm sorry, Dad,' she told them inadequately several times during that long period when she stayed in her room. 'It was like being under a spell. I didn't know what I was doing.'

All her mother would say in reply was: 'Now you'll never, ever do anything like that again, will you, Alison.'

'No, Mum, no – I won't.'

'Now you promise.'

'Honestly, Mum, yes, I promise.'

Her father seemed to understand rather better how she felt. But he couldn't change his nature.

'If we seem a bit calm to you, Alison,' he said, 'it's because we never really gave up hope. We never really believed you were dead. That's why we wouldn't go to the Minster.

'We never dreamt you'd be with that woman, but we felt you'd turn up somewhere, somehow.'

Alison embraced them several times and the Allbrights weren't normally a demonstrative family.

She didn't want to face anybody at school again, ever. She had made fools of them all but a still bigger one of herself. Especially she didn't want to see Raine who, her mother told her, had kept on calling.

She spent most of the time gazing out of the window. Her mind played with curious thoughts. It had occurred to her, for instance, how alike she and Mrs Considine had been in some ways while directly opposite in others. Almost as if they had been mirror images of each other.

It was a thought which took hold of her and for many hours she would sit analysing just how many similarities and differences there had been.

And then, at ten past four one afternoon, after spending four days in her room, Alison suddenly appeared downstairs, fully dressed. Keith and her mother were having tea. Her mother looked at her hopefully.

'What day is it?' asked Alison. 'Have you just come back from school, Keith?'

'It's Friday,' said Keith, 'but I haven't been. They've let me have a few days off.'

'And you took it? That's not like you. You'll never get to Oxford this way.'

'What?'

'It doesn't matter.'

'Sit down and have some tea, love,' said Mrs Allbright.

That afternoon, Alison had had a sort of revelation. It was a very simple one and she couldn't think now why she hadn't had it before. It had come to her when she had been going over in her mind, yet again, everything that Raine had said to her at the party at Rosewilder.

At the time, that conversation had filled her almost with horror. She had wanted to forget about it as quickly as possible. But now she realized she had been stupid.

As Alison ate, her mother took Mrs Considine's gifts out of the cupboard and laid them on the sideboard.

'These are worth a lot of money,' she said. 'Mrs Lawlor told me. We don't really know what to do with them, whether it would be bad taste to sell them and buy some furniture.'

'I should give them to charity,' said Alison. 'If people don't like our furniture they needn't come here.'

'Inverted snob,' muttered Keith.

She looked at him with some suspicion. His face was bent downwards but she could see there was a curve to his lip.

She and Keith might get on together yet.

'You're feeling a bit better, are you, dear?' asked her mother, sitting down. 'You think you might be ready to go to school again soon?'

'I – ' Alison started to say something, then paused. 'Maybe.'

'There's somebody at the door,' said Mrs Allbright, rising again.

It was Raine, straight from school. She burst in, glowing with health. It was the first time Alison had seen her in that house. She looked thoroughly at home.

'And about time, too,' said Raine. 'Come on. You're going out for a walk, isn't she, Mrs Allbright? It's lovely outside.'

Alison allowed herself to be yanked out into Holtwood Lane.

'Where shall we go?' asked Raine. 'Is there anywhere nice around here?'

'What about the quarry?' said Alison, dully. 'It's along this way.' They walked down the lane and Alison squinted at Raine out of the corner of her eye.

'Don't jolly me along, Raine,' she said. 'I want to know what everybody thinks. You and the people at school.'

154

'Opinions are mixed,' replied Raine, suddenly wryly serious. 'Some people think you're a dangerous lunatic, some are quite admiring, some think this shows there's a lot more to you than anybody thought, some couldn't care less and some . . .

'Well, to be honest, there are some people with a well-developed sense of humour who think it's the funniest thing that ever happened. That's putting it all quite straight.'

'What about Mr Craig?'

'He's got his second chance, hasn't he? It's what he said he wanted. It'll be interesting to see how he makes out, won't it.'

That had been said very seriously but when Alison glanced at Raine out of the corner of her eye again she saw that Raine was looking back at her quite mischievously, almost as if she wanted to laugh.

They had reached the rusty metal gate to the quarry. Raine paused.

'So are you going to pluck up courage? Monday morning? Or can't you face school yet?'

Alison laid her arms along the top rail of the gate and stared into the distance.

'Could you still envy the Allbrights?' she asked, unexpectedly. 'Do you still think they're truly alive?'

'Envy –' echoed Raine, momentarily puzzled. 'Oh! What I said at the party. You're trying to embarrass me, are you, Alison?'

Alison continued to stare into the distance.

'You're taking an unfair advantage and making me blush,' said Raine, 'but yes. I don't suppose you believe that but – '

'Oh, I believe you. I didn't then but I do now. Everything you said was true.'

Alison fell silent. Then she looked at Raine and said:

'You've told me what the other people at school think about me. But you still haven't said what *you* think.'

For reply, Raine made a face and after a moment Alison smiled at her. It was a shy little smile, quite charming in its way, not morose at all.

'Then I'll go back to school Monday and I'll try not to be impossible, Raine. I don't think I will be but kick me if I am.'

'Are you never going to stop embarrassing me?' asked Raine as Alison pushed at the gate. She followed her through and closed it behind her. 'You mean it about going back to school on Monday? You're not scared any more?'

The old Alison would have been scared.

'I'm looking forward to it. I want to see their faces. It's a marvellous feeling. I've never had a feeling like this before.'

The feeling was of freedom. She didn't care what any of them thought. They'd all, even including Raine, come down to size. She could even feel a little sorry for some of them. Jenny Allingham, for instance. She had never had anything to say in Jenny Allingham's company and had always taken it for granted that it was her fault. But perhaps it wasn't. Perhaps it was Jenny Allingham's.

Alison kicked off her sandals. Then, just as once she had twirled for joy on the lawns of Rosewilder, now she began to twirl like a ballerina on the rough, tussocky grass beside the quarry.

'You'll hurt your feet,' called Raine, astonished at such exuberance. Alison had never been an exuberant person. 'There are stones.'

But Alison merely laughed. The grass, though rough, was warm and springy and inviting to the feet.

Then, for the first time, Raine glanced round at the quarry.

'This is marvellous,' she said suddenly, 'absolutely marvellous.'

A weird little world of its own, silent except for droning bees and whirring crickets. A forgotten landscape of miniature hills and glens and lakes.

'We could be in another world,' cried Raine, enchanted, and Alison stopped her twirling and, picking up her sandals, followed her barefooted into the heart of it.

'Oh, Alison, I never knew there was anything like this near here. You know how I love wild places.

'Everything around Sturridge is so neat and tidy and the one decent bit of heathland there used to be they've turned into a stupid country park and picnic area. I didn't know there was this. Oh, look! That's a dragonfly. I've only ever seen one once before.'

The dragonfly shimmered, metallic blue-green, over one of the pools.

'Oh, Alison, you've had this wonderful place at the end of your lane all this time. Why didn't you ever tell me?'

FIRST TERM AT TREBIZON
Anne Digby

At last – a new series of boarding school stories to delight a new generation of readers. In this first story, Rebecca Mason is plunged into life at Trebizon, a famous school for girls. Lonely, afraid and anxious to prove herself, she determines to write something that will be accepted for publication in the special jubilee edition of the school magazine but the piece that appears is not the one she intended . . .

BOSS OF THE POOL
Robin Klein

The last thing Shelley wanted was to have to spend her evenings at the hostel when all her friends were going away for the summer holidays – all because her mother, who worked there, wouldn't let her stay in the house on her own. Then to her horror, mentally handicapped Ben attaches himself to her from the start and although he's terrified of the pool, he comes to watch her swimming. Despite herself, Shelley begins to help him overcome his fear.

ROB'S PLACE
John Rowe Townsend

Everyone Rob cares for is deserting him: first his dad left, then his best friend, and even his mum hasn't time for him now she has a new husband and baby. Just when he thinks he's got a special friend in Mike it turns out that he's leaving too. But it's through Mike that Rob learns how to escape from his everyday life – he discovers a fantastic place which is all his own and where he is master. But can he control his fantasy or will his Paradise become a nightmare?